Kurt d'Estier held the Martin family fortunes in the palm of his hand—so it was
going to make things difficult, to say the
least, when Mrs Martin's son Colin ran
off with Kurt's fiancée. So Mrs Martin
persuaded her secretary Maxine Martin
—no relation—to pretend to be her
daughter, another Maxine, and go off to
Morocco to try to pacify Kurt. Maxine could hardly refuse—but then she
didn't know what a hornet's nest she
was about to bring down on her head!

THE DARK OASIS

BY

MARGARET PARGETER

MILLS & BOON LIMITED
15–16 BROOK'S MEWS
LONDON W1A 1DR

First published 1980
Australian copyright 1980
Philippine copyright 1980
This edition 1980

© Margaret Pargeter 1980

ISBN 0 263 73349 1

Set in Linotype Pilgrim 10 on 10½ pt.

Made and printed in Great Britain by
Richard Clay (The Chaucer Press), Ltd., Bungay, Suffolk

CHAPTER ONE

FOR a whole day Maxine Martin had waited in Casablanca for some form of acknowledgement from Kurt d'Estier, and none came. It wasn't until the morning of the second day that his secretary rang back to say she had managed to get in touch with him, and he would be quite willing to see Miss Martin at an arranged rendez-vous.

'*Merci*.' Maxine remained polite only with difficulty. She hoped the secretary wouldn't detect her sarcasm as she told her she was most kind. '*Vous êtes très amiable*.'

'Not at all, *mademoiselle*,' the secretary assured her smoothly, in excellent English, which Maxine suspected was meant to demonstrate without words exactly what she thought of Maxine's halting French.

'Where do I see Monsieur d'Estier?' asked Maxine, seeing no sense in prolonging the conversation. 'I realise he—he must have a lot on his mind at the moment, but I hope he doesn't intend keeping me waiting much longer?'

'No, no, of course not.' The secretary's voice was still smooth. From it Maxine was unable to guess whether she was aware of the sudden misfortune which had struck Kurt d'Estier or not. 'But I'm afraid Mademoiselle must be prepared to make the journey to his *ksar*, as he cannot see you in Casa.'

'Casa?'

'*Je vous demande pardon, mademoiselle*. I mean Casablanca.'

'I see.' Again Maxine felt foolish, and again reacting

sensitively, wondered if this had been intended. She went on quickly, glad the secretary couldn't see her pink cheeks, 'How do I get there, then? I'm afraid I have no idea where Monsieur d'Estier lives.'

'He has several homes, *mademoiselle*,' the voice of efficiency purred on. 'He is at present at his castle in the High Atlas, and if you would leave at once for Marra-kesh, he will arrange for you to be picked up at the airport.'

Uncertainly, Maxine's brow furrowed. This was some thing she hadn't been prepared for. Mrs Martin, Maxine's employer of the same name as herself, had been insistent that there would be no need to go any further than Casablanca, where she was now.

The secretary, taking Maxine's consent for granted, proceeded to give her a time of departure, assuring her that a taxi would be sent immediately to take her to the plane.

When Maxine murmured, 'Thank you,' rather dazedly, the woman said sharply, 'I should advise you not to keep Monsieur d'Estier waiting. He is a very busy man and doesn't appreciate those who waste his time.'

Hot with indignation, Maxine stammered, 'I have no intention of doing that.'

'Then that will be all, *mademoiselle*. *Au revoir*,' and the paragon at the other end hung up, without giving Maxine a chance to reply.

'Goodbye, yourself!' Maxine muttered, on a wave of youthful frustration, banging down the dead receiver. Uneasily she wondered what the woman was called. When Maxine had asked to speak to Kurt d'Estier yesterday, in the huge business complex where Mrs Martin said she would find him, she had been put through to his secretary, but the woman hadn't given her name, although Maxine had asked. Obviously Kurt d'Estier would only employ those as devious as himself!

Oh, well, as she wasn't likely to be speaking to his

secretary again, it couldn't matter that the woman seemed to despise her. Ruefully Maxine paused to glance briefly around the extremely smart hotel bedroom. It was perhaps foolish to hope that Monsieur d'Estier's primitive castle would be as comfortable as one of the best hotels on the Avenue des Forces Armées Royales, but as he was unlikely to ask her to stay she could be back here this evening. After all, he wouldn't seek to prolong an interview with a girl who he probably believed to be the sister of the man who had run off with his fiancé!

Quickly, keeping in mind the need to hurry, she thrust a few toilet items into a copious shoulder-bag. Her clothes she would leave behind, in the room. She hadn't brought much as she hadn't expected to be in Morocco for more than a couple of days, at the most—no longer than it took to make a brief but personal apology, on Mrs Martin's behalf, to Kurt d'Estier, because of the dreadful thing Colin had done. Mrs Martin had been tearfully insistent. It was the personal touch which made all the difference, she said, and in view of the gravity of the situation nothing else, in this case, would suffice.

An hour later, sitting in the plane for Marrakesh, Maxine felt her anxiety growing. After some careful thought, she had tried to get in touch with Mrs Martin to ask her advice, but failed. At the last moment, with her courage almost failing her, she hadn't been sure she was doing the right thing, but as the operator hadn't been able to raise a reply from Mrs Martin's London home, Maxine had decided unhappily that she must just go ahead as planned. Yet, for all she had managed to scrape together enough courage, she had needed every bit of it to board this plane. It hadn't made anything any easier to realise she had no alternative but to make this final attempt to see Kurt d'Estier. Why, she wondered, with bleak despair, had Colin Martin chosen to elope with the French fiancée of the man who apparently held the Martin fortunes in the palm of his arrogant hand? Maxine had only seen Colin Martin a few times since she had come to work for his mother, but she knew he often angered his mother by doing stupid things. This latest escapade of his, however, crowned the lot! It also made Maxine wonder how she had ever allowed herself to get mixed up with such a family.

To try to divert herself, in order to retain a fast slipping composure, Maxine let her thoughts drift back over the last few years. Her parents had died, but her father had left enough money for her to live and be educated at the convent. Mrs Martin had known about Maxine from the beginning, as she took a great interest in the convent, since her own daughter, of exactly the same name as Maxine, had been educated there. Mrs Martin's daughter, being ten years older than Maxine, had left almost before Maxine started, and Maxine had never known her. But when this daughter had married, in Mexico, against her mother's wishes, and vowed she was never coming back, Mrs Martin had immediately asked Maxine to come and live with her.

The Reverend Mother had talked to Maxine before she had been allowed to make up her mind. 'Ever since Mrs Martin discovered you had exactly the same name as her daughter, as well as a distinct resemblance, she has been intrigued. Now that her own daughter has defied her by marrying a man Mrs Martin doesn't approve of, I believe she sees in you a kind of substitute daughter, which might not be a good thing, my child.'

'She does need a personal secretary,' Maxine had protested.

'Certainly,' the Reverend Mother had agreed, her old eyes dwelling with gentle affection on a girl she had come to love. 'I find it rather difficult to explain, but I would rather you developed your own personality in your own time, rather than be forced into the mould of another girl. I can understand Mrs Martin's feelings,' she continued dryly. 'Since her daughter decided to go blonde, you look almost exactly alike. For years, now, she has been small and fair, like you, and although she is considerably older, modern make-up can effectively disguise this. Unless one takes the trouble to look closely.'

Eventually the Reverend Mother had been persuaded and, just over a year ago, a month or two before her nineteenth birthday, Maxine had gone to live with Mrs Martin. It had been the promise of a proper home, after years in an institution, which Maxine had found irresistible. She hadn't been there long, though, before she came to realise there had been a lot of truth in what the Reverend Mother had tried to tell her.

Mrs Martin's pride in her daughter, which had been almost phenomenal before she had married, had suffered a severe blow. With Maxine quickly established in her London home, few people realised, because Mrs Martin, despite her huge business interests, was something of a recluse, that Maxine wasn't her real daughter. And, especially as she had asked Maxine not to draw attention to this, over the year she had been with her it had worked tolerably well.

Even Mrs Martin's son, her only other child, who looked after her business interests in Morocco had joined in the pretence. Rather jokingly, admittedly, but on the odd occasion Maxine had seen him, he had seemed grateful that anything had helped his mother over the unhappiness of his sister's departure. Now it was ironic that Colin had committed almost the same offence himself, although his, Maxine considered, was much worse. So far as she could make out, his sister's Mexican cowboy hadn't belonged to anyone else.

Mrs Martin had invested large sums of money in industrial schemes in Casablanca, but exactly how Kurt d'Estier came into it, Maxine still wasn't sure. She did know that he held a controlling interest in most of the companies, and that he could make or break Mrs Martin, practically overnight. It seemed incredible that, aware of this, Colin had gone off with the man's beautiful French fiancée.

'Oh, the fool, the fool!' Mrs Martin had wept, her rather heavy face white when she'd learnt the news. 'It will be the end of me, Maxine. However did I come to have such children? Why ever did I listen to Colin in the first place? Invest, he said. Sell out here and invest over there. Now, if Kurt d'Estier chooses, and I don't see why he shouldn't after this, he can break me!'

Money, Maxine had realised for some time, was to Mrs Martin very important, the most important thing in her life. It astonished and dismayed Maxine that she appeared more concerned by the possible loss of it than what might happen to Colin when Kurt d'Estier found him.

'Surely this Monsieur d'Estier wouldn't revenge himself on you, a helpless woman, who had nothing to do with what's happened?' Maxine had suggested, 'And his fiancée must be partly to blame, at least. I'm sure Colin couldn't have carried her off if she hadn't been willing.'

'You don't know Kurt d'Estier,' Mrs Martin had retorted sharply, 'or you wouldn't ask. He has no great opinion of a business woman—or any woman, I think, come to that. I don't doubt he was marrying this woman simply to provide himself with a son and heir, someone to leave his considerable wealth to, and I'm very sure that if he fails to find her he'll seek revenge.'

'This is the twentieth century!' Maxine had gasped.

'Not in some parts of the world,' Mrs Martin had declared darkly. 'Not as we know it, anyway. Kurt d'Estier has mixed blood in his veins. Mostly French, I believe, but somewhere, Colin heard, there's Berber ancestry. It's even rumoured that he's entitled to call himself a Sheik, which may be nonsense, but he does have great influence. And, being no more than thirty-five or six, he still has the energy to make the most of it.'

Maxine had sought helplessly to comfort her distressed employer. 'If he isn't a man of principle, Mrs Martin, there's always the law, which might help.'

'The law!' Mrs Martin all but spat. 'You'd soon see what would happen if we tried to enforce that. Of course the man is clever enough not to break it. If Colin doesn't come back, I don't think I'd dare face him. From all accounts he's a barbarian, in spite of his international business reputation.'

'Have you ever met him?' Maxine asked weakly, scarcely able to envisage a man such as Mrs Martin described.

'Yes, once. You know my reluctance to leave the country, but once, a few years ago, my daughter and I went to Casablanca and met him briefly. Max, as we call my daughter, had just had her hair freshly tinted,' Mrs Martin had sighed, as if not sure whether the recollection of this pleased or upset her. 'I thought she looked very beautiful.'

'Did she like Monsieur d'Estier, do you think?'

'I think she found him attractive, but then most women do.'

Maxine had persisted, why she wasn't sure, 'And what did he think of your daughter, Mrs Martin? If he was looking for a wife, wouldn't she have been suitable?'

To Maxine's surprise, as she hadn't expected Mrs Martin to take her remark seriously, her employer had nodded her head. 'Exactly what I thought. Such an alliance would certainly have cemented our mutual interests, but although he took her out once or twice nothing ever came of it. When I asked Max about it, she would only say she found him too domineering, that a girl would have to subjugate her whole personality if she married a man like that.'

'It makes one wonder,' Maxine had frowned, 'how his fiancée ever escaped him.'

'I can't understand it,' Mrs Martin agreed. 'Of course

Colin is good-looking and much more human, I think, than Kurt d'Estier. Not,' she added, white-faced and anxious, 'that this excuses him from possibly ruining me!'

A shiver had ran through Maxine then, one of dark premonition as she had gazed at Mrs Martin. 'You've asked me to go to Casablanca, but wouldn't it be better if you went yourself?'

'No!' Mrs Martin had exclaimed hysterically. 'You know my nerves won't allow me to leave the country. Foreign travel has always terrified me, I just can't do it any more. I would collapse, especially on a mission such as this. I've never asked you to do anything out of the ordinary before, Maxine, and I've tried to be kind.'

'Please, don't upset yourself,' Maxine had broken in because, despite her faults, Mrs Martin had been the kindest employer possible, treating her almost as she had done her daughter. 'Of course I'll go, but you'll have to tell me exactly what to say. I've had no experience of dealing with men like Monsieur d'Estier. I haven't even been abroad yet.'

The relief on Mrs Martin's face should have been re-ward in itself. 'You don't have to say anything. I just want you to carry a personal apology. I'll write the letter immediately, offering my condolences, and willingness to help in any way I can. It's the only thing which might make any difference. It's too easy to pick up a telephone, and he knows it. No, I must either go myself, which I can't do, or send my daughter.'

'But I'm not your daughter, Mrs Martin!'

'He doesn't know that.' Mrs Martin, seeing Maxine's instant alarm, had become hectoring. 'Fortunately, when Max ran away, I forbade Colin to mention it to Kurt d'Estier, as I still had hopes in that direction, should Max come to her senses. I have reason to believe that Monsieur d'Estier still doesn't know Max is in Mexico.'

Maxine stirred in her seat on the plane, remembering

her continuing uneasiness. 'Which means I would have to lie.'

'No. All you have to do is not deny anything. If you think about it, Maxine, my dear, you'll soon get the hang of it. He'll simply assume, because you look so much like my daughter and it's years since he saw her, that you're Max. All I'm asking you to do is let him! You'll only be with him a short time, and if he believes I've sent someone close to me, then he'll be convinced I'm sincere.'

'If,' Maxine faltered, 'he has such influence, how is it that Monsieur d'Estier hasn't caught up with Colin and his runaway fiancée?'

'You forget,' Mrs Martin had snapped impatiently, 'that Colin has been in Morocco a long time. He knows the country well. He can also plan fairly well, when he sets his mind to it. This girl whom he's gone off with belongs to a wealthy family and her parents live in France. For all I know they could be there.'

'Her family would surely not welcome them there?' Maxine had questioned, shocked.

'Probably not,' Mrs Martin groaned, covering her face with her hands. 'How is it?' she added bitterly, 'that the best of parents often seem burdened with the worst children!'

Knowing something of Mrs Martin, after working for her for so long, Maxine had wondered wryly if things might not have turned out a little differently if she had cared for her children as much as her business. Yet Mrs Martin did suffer over them, anyone could see this last escapade of Colin's had left her very low. Maxine had seen how such a trip to Morocco could be too much, at this time, for the ageing Mrs Martin.

'Don't worry,' Maxine had heard herself saying, 'just leave everything to me. After all, Monsieur d'Estier can't do much more than perhaps express his anger. And, if

he happens to be heartbroken, he might not even do
this.'

Maxine thought now that it must surely have been
rather peculiar that neither she nor Mrs Martin had stopped to spare a few pitying thoughts for Kurt d'Estier
over the loss of his bride-to-be. Perhaps it had been Mrs
Martin's disparaging remarks about him which had
effectively dispersed the sympathy in Maxine's heart, but
even the strongest men, she supposed, must have at least
one chink in their armour, if only one of pride.

Still feeling doubtful but managing to hide it, Maxine
had taken the first plane from Gatwick, after Mrs
Martin had ensured, through her London office, that
Monsieur d'Estier was willing to see her personal repre-
sentative. Maxine had had no idea whether she should
be reassured or otherwise by this condescension. She had
only known she felt very young and apprehensive, and
not at all looking forward to what could only be at the
best a very uncomfortable interview.

In Casablanca, the great seaport and industrial centre
of Morocco's west coast, Maxine had expected she would
have little else to do, but to see Kurt d'Estier briefly before returning to England. She had no reason to suppose
he would ask her to stay, to help him in his search for
the missing pair. She didn't know the man, but she
could imagine his sarcasm, if she were to even offer.
With compassion in her heart for Mrs Martin, she did
wish there had been something she could do, and she
did hope she could, at least, bring home better news of
some kind. Vaguely she had dreamt of finding Monsieur
d'Estier's fiancée back in Casablanca again, restored to
his safe keeping.

But in Casablanca, in spite of repeated attempts, Maxine had been unable to contact Monsieur d'Estier, and
now, it seemed, she must journey almost into the desert
if she wanted to complete her mission.

At Marrakesh, almost two hundred miles away, she

found, as the secretary had promised, a car waiting for her. In charge was a swarthy, silent driver who bore her off immediately. When she asked, '*Parlez-vous anglais, monsieur?*' he replied, 'Yes.' But if he did understand English, he appeared to be able to say little else. To all her other questions he merely smiled politely.

After this, although she tried, she could get nothing out of him, and decided to concentrate on the scenery. She already knew that Marrakesh was one of the three imperial cities of Morocco. It was a huge, flat-looking city, set on the wide, fertile Haouz Plain, with huge palm groves stretching to the east and north. In the background, their tops still gleaming white from the winter snows, were the high peaks of the High Atlas, that great chain of mountains which ran like a backbone down through the country.

The road on which they travelled was good until they reached the mountains, where it deteriorated rapidly. The car sped over potholes on what seemed unsurfaced track, as they left the main highway, the driver appearing as unconcerned for the vehicle's springs as he was for his passenger. Sand infiltrated with a fine dust, nearly choking her, but it became quite clear that the driver hadn't been instructed to give her any special care or attention, for he rarely slowed down.

As dusk approached, the sky changed from the daytime violet through to purple, then the deepest indigo. Over the western horizon the sun went down in a blaze of gold, leaving great streaks of amethyst to flush crimson before fading to grey as night fell and the stars came out. For hours they drove, Maxine growing more and more uncomfortable, with her mouth parched and her thin cotton suit sticking to her hot, perspiring body. When she felt so weary she doubted if she could stand it much longer, they arrived at a large castle.

Maxine thought it looked like a castle, but as it was dark and there were few lights she wasn't too sure. The tall shapes of palm trees were etched against the sky and there was darker foliage, the compact shape behind this suggesting a building of some size, but it was difficult to tell. Then they swept through a huge archway, set in a massive wall, and came to a stop.

The castle, if this was what it was, looked primitive. As Maxine stumbled, unhelped, from the car, her eyes, grown accustomed to the darkness, saw how it reared above her, a fortress of rough, hard stone. In the courtyard, where she stood, the entrance was at one corner, a corner which she noticed angled into a tower with slit-shaped window openings, as though it was used, or had been used as some kind of fortress.

What, Maxine wondered, fear such as she had never known gripping her by her throat, was she to encounter here, in this savage looking place, so far removed from civilisation?

The driver, with a rough gesture, waved her inside and, still stumbling, she followed him. The interior was a little better, with attractive plasterwork and cool marble floors, but the simplicity of it was such that it gave no hint of a welcome. Again Maxine found herself shivering and had to make an effort to hang on to her fast slipping self-possession.

'If you will come this way, *mademoiselle*?'

Startled, Maxine almost jumped, in spite of being so tired. She hadn't noticed that the driver had been replaced by a white-coated servant. He was older, this man, and his expression was quite kind. With a flicker of relief, she turned to him. At least he was an improvement on the one who had brought her here.

Quickly she asked, 'Are you taking me to see Monsieur d'Estier?' She hadn't meant to sound so abrupt and felt ashamed, but the servant apparently didn't see anything wrong in her attitude.

He bowed again. 'I will take you to your room, *mademoiselle*,' he said.

'Thank you,' Maxine managed, 'but I would like to see Monsieur at once. You understand?'

The man hesitated, frowning a little, 'A thousand pardons, *mademoiselle*, but my master is not here.'

'Not here!' Maxine's hopes of returning to Marrakesh that evening faded. All at once she felt too small, too vulnerable and had to fight down a growing fear. 'Then have I come to the wrong place?'

'No, *mademoiselle*, I did not mean that. My master is out. He will return very soon, but at the moment he is not here.'

'I see.' The painstaking speech of the servant tried her patience, but she could see there was nothing to be gained by protesting further. The man had obviously been warned that Mademoiselle might prove fractious after her journey. He looked as unmovable as stone.

Without another word of protest, she followed him up the marble staircase, through archways which led to the bedrooms, feeling everything was so unreal that any minute she might wake up and find she had been dreaming. Putting out tentative fingers, she touched the rough, plastered wall, and was quickly assured this was no dream but stark reality!

The bedroom she was shown to was, to her surprise, spacious and comfortable, the low divan covered with silken rugs and cushions, with thick woven rugs on the floor. Through the open door of the adjoining room, Maxine could see a bath.

'If Mademoiselle will remain here, I will send Vega to you. She will help you to prepare for when the Sidi returns.'

'No!' Maxine replied quickly. Then, as the man paused impassively, 'There's no need. I would rather manage on my own. I didn't even bring a change of clothing, so I can only wash.'

'All the same, *mademoiselle*, the Sidi commands you have Vega, so she will come.'

Bowing, he departed leaving Maxine biting her lip while apprehension gnawed holes in her stomach. Since coming to Morocco, every decision had been taken out of her hands. First the secretary, then the driver and this last man seemed to treat her like a puppet. Now there was to be a girl servant who would probably expect to wash and dress her as though she were a child. After this she might be granted an audience with the great Sidi or Monsieur—whatever his real title was, if he wasn't too tired from his travels to see her! With a sob of angry frustration, replacing fright, Maxine wished heartily that she was back in London, where she belonged.

The clothes she had on were hot and sticky and, her temper subsiding, she felt irritated that she hadn't brought at least one dress to change into. If she had had any sense she might have realised she could be delayed. Even in England this could have happened, and how long could she possibly live in one dress?

All of a sudden she shivered, hearing the night wind moaning around the ancient walls, bringing with it such a feeling of loneliness that she almost cried out. She had always been sensitive to atmosphere, but never could she remember responding as dramatically as she did now. A nameless dread filled her as she stood there, along with a peculiar excitement. It was as if the future beckoned yet repelled, urged her on while the reins of a soberly conventional upbringing held her back. She had a sense of standing at a crossroads, having no clear idea of which direction she wished to take. Her mind was fused in a fog of indecision, as every instinct warned her to flee this place before its absent master returned!

It took the sound of her own quickly drawn breath to bring Maxine to her senses, making her immediately conscious how easily she might terrify herself with such foolish fancies. Kurt d'Estier might naturally feel like putting her to a little inconvenience, but wouldn't it be sensible to suppose he would do his best to get rid of someone like herself as soon as possible, rather than keep her here during what must surely be a very unhappy period of his life?

Shrugging her slim shoulders, reassured by such sensible thoughts, she went more confidently into the bathroom. Though it was far from luxurious, there was a bath. Doubtfully she stared at the taps, as if undecided whether or not there would be water to fill it, in such an arid country. Then a girl appeared in the doorway.

'I am Vega.' The girl smiled as she introduced herself.

Maxine already knew her name, but she didn't say anything. Fearing it would be useless to protest again that she didn't need a servant, she gazed at Vega rather helplessly.

'I will run your bath, *mademoiselle*.' Vega, not obviously disturbed by Maxine's silence, held out a thin robe. 'Izaak speaks that Mademoiselle has forgotten to bring clothes, but we have enough here. If Mademoiselle will undress and bath, I will help to prepare her for my master.'

There it was again, the impression that she was here as a kind of living sacrifice for the enjoyment of their revered master! She managed a weak but determined smile at Vega, whose large, patient brown eyes betrayed only a desire to please. 'I will certainly have a bath, but I intend wearing my own clothes again.'

The water was warm and pleasant and she enjoyed her bath more than she could ever remember enjoying a bath before. Ruefully she realised just how pampered an existence she had become used to. Vega filled the bath with scented oils, which she explained in her broken English were made from herbs and a secret recipe. Whatever the recipe, Maxine knew she had never felt so relaxed, and wondered vaguely if she might steal it to take home with her.

She might have lingered in the bath longer if Vega hadn't been there, the wish for privacy that she had

expressed having been smilingly ignored. She felt uncomfortable at the way in which the girl, for all her
meek appearance, quickly took charge, seizing and washing her gilt-gold hair as though it was something too
rare to be left covered with sand and dust.

'Mademoiselle is beautiful and very young,' Vega's
brown eyes dwelt impersonally but warmly on Maxine's
slender, shapely body, the pale, silken hair which hung
long and thick almost down to her waist. 'My master
will like you very much, Vega thinks.'

Maxine's soft, violet grey eyes cooled, her full, pink
mouth tightening. No one had ever said she was beautiful before, but her odd flare of pleasure faded at the
girl's last remark. 'I'm sure Monsieur d'Estier will not
mind how I look,' she replied stiffly, wrapping herself
tighter in the huge fluffy bath towel while Vega industriously dried her hair. 'I expect to be leaving tomorrow,
Vega, so his opinion cannot matter.'

'When visitors come to the house of Sidi Kurt,' the
girl laughed softly, 'they sometimes do not leave for a
very long time.'

Those whom Vega talked of would be women, Maxine
decided scornfully. In a desert stronghold, such as this,
Monsieur d'Estier might feel free to indulge in vices his
fiancée knew nothing about. Thinking of his fiancée
brought a twinge of shame. Perhaps, even now, he was
out looking for her. Sometimes it didn't do to judge too
hastily, before one knew all the facts.

The picture of a desperately weary man searching for
his lost bride suddenly filled Maxine with compassion,
again making her wonder why neither she nor Mrs
Martin had thought of this, instead of being so critical
of Kurt d'Estier. If he loved his fiancée, he was probably
half out of his mind. In such circumstances, he could
surely be excused if his treatment of the girl who he
supposed was the criminal's sister left much to be desired.

After Vega finished drying and combing her hair,

Maxine dressed once more in her cotton suit. She left off the jacket as the top was brief but adequate and the night was still warm. The silken djellaba which Véga held out she refused, ignoring the girl's dismayed expression. It would never do to appear relaxed and overdressed, on what must be considered a formal, impersonal occasion. If she was to present Mrs Martin's letter, it would be better done in a businesslike fashion.

Using a little of the make-up she had brought with her helped steady her jumping nerves, as that interview loomed frighteningly nearer. Her hair she coiled neatly again at the back of her head, not realising that the style, though formal, made her look younger than ever. Her eyes, unnaturally large, partly through strain, seemed to dominate her youthful face, and her skin had a pearly, translucent quality which made the soft curves of her full mouth seem wholly vulnerable.

At last she was ready and, with Vega in close attendance, left the room to go downstairs. Vega had brought Maxine some mint tea, which she had found very refreshing, but she felt extremely hungry and hoped it would not be long before she was offered at least something light to eat. Unhappily she was aware that she shouldn't be taking anything for granted. Kurt d'Estier might not feel generous enough to feed the girl who he would believe to be Colin Martin's sister.

They were almost at the bottom of the stairs when the outer door was flung open and through it strode a man. Too dumbfounded to take another step, Maxine froze, staring at him. Everything inside her was paralysed. Never could she recall feeling like it before. This must be the impact she had once read about, that of a desert man on a stranger. As his head came up sharply and she met his dark eyes, a shiver of fright ran through her nerves like lightning, making her limbs shake.

Coming to an abrupt halt, the man returned Maxine's startled stare grimly, his eyes narrowed. 'Mademoiselle?'

His voice was clipped, grim. It, too, she was dismayed to find, had its effect. It played on her senses, like fingers strumming a highly tuned instrument, making her immediately as taut as a violin string.

'Good evening.' Maxine's voice trembled slightly, and though she tried to keep her cool her eyes widened on the man in front of her. He was clad in a white burnous, which swung from his wide, powerful shoulders, and on his head he wore a white haik, held in place by narrow ropes. Beneath it his face was hard and hawk-like, his figure tall and strong. He must be one of Kurt d'Estier's men. Faintly she hoped she wouldn't meet many more like him.

'I'm—I'm waiting to see Monsieur d'Estier,' she got out at last, with an effort which must have betrayed something of her inner agitation.

With a sudden cruel smile he bore down on her, his eyes flashing sardonically to her trembling hands. 'You fail to recognise me, then, Mademoiselle Martin? Of course it is some time ago, and you haven't seen me dressed like this. Or is it that the years have changed me considerably more than they appear to have changed you?'

Feeling completely devastated, Maxine clutched a near-by support as a wave of terror hit her. The touch of hard wood helped bring her to her senses, and afterwards she felt grateful that her intelligence, which the good nuns had always praised, hadn't let her down. So this was Kurt d'Estier! Now was the time to confess that she hadn't recognised him because, contrary to what he thought, they had not met before. But the moment of opportunity passed, never to present itself so easily again, as Mrs Martin's strict instructions proved too strong for Maxine to ignore.

'I'm very sorry, Monsieur d'Estier.' Lifting her chin a little, she managed to smile lightly, which she hoped would hide her inner apprehension. 'As you say, a costume like the one you're wearing makes an excellent disguise. You're quite right, I'm afraid I didn't recognise you.'

CHAPTER TWO

KURT D'ESTIER paused, his eyes fixed on Maxine's face. 'It is not a costume I am wearing, Miss Martin.' His voice, which had been cool, turned colder.

Maxine flushed uncomfortably. 'No,' she stammered, scarcely conscious of what she was saying, 'I'm sorry. I just didn't expect to find you wearing such clothes.'

'I have every right to. Don't be so quick to jump to the wrong conclusions.'

He didn't explain further. Instead his hand came out to grasp her chin, to turn her face up to him as he towered above her. 'I take it for granted,' he said, 'that the years have changed me, but you, *mademoiselle*, appear younger than I would ever have believed possible. I find it hard to believe you must be almost— thirty?'

A tremor ran through her as she lowered her gaze, so he shouldn't detect her dismay. Mrs Martin had been so sure Kurt d'Estier wouldn't remember her daughter, other than vaguely. To have to pose as a much older woman and at the same time, by means of half truths, to give the impression of really being Mrs Martin's daughter wasn't going to be easy—especially now that she had met Kurt d'Estier and learnt something of what she could be up against. However had Mrs Martin imagined she could hoodwink a man like this? This tall, dark, hawk-like man, his face full of unsmiling menace, was far outside the range of her limited experience. There was about him a bitter, brooding ruthlessness, a cold vitality, which Maxine found frightening.

Swallowing hard on the lump in her throat, she whispered unhappily, 'There are many ways by which a woman might keep her youthful appearance, *monsieur*.'

'So it would seem,' he agreed suavely, yet Maxine saw how his eyes narrowed again and his nostrils tensed, like those of a well-bred stallion. His eyes appeared to strip her naked, as though there were no secrets about her he hadn't known. Her heart thudding heavily because of the direction her too vivid imagination was taking her, she lowered her betraying eyes.

As she felt him continuing to stare, it came to her that the conversation was perhaps somewhat incredible, considering the gravity of the situation. Her mission hadn't even been mentioned yet.

'Have you been out looking for your—your fiancée?' she faltered, too mixed up to approach the subject in a more diplomatic fashion, but very aware that she had none of the finesse an older, more experienced person might have had.

'Have you come all the way here just to ask that?' he countered harshly.

She flushed at the direct snub, delivered with such marked sarcasm, but felt more annoyed with herself that she had forgotten her carefully rehearsed opening gambit, one which she had been repeating over and over again, ever since she had boarded the plane at Gatwick. 'I'm extremely sorry, *monsieur*,' she began formally. 'Mrs Martin and I are fully aware of your troubles, and I have with me a personal letter of apology. Mrs Martin sent me with it—she felt it was the least she could do.' Quickly, very conscious of his grim silence, she took the letter from her handbag, almost thrusting it at him.

Without replying he accepted the missive from her shaking hands and tore it immediately in two. Before

Maxine's horrified gaze he threw it away from him, his movements deliberate and coldly contemptuous.

The letter, which had given Mrs Martin so much trouble to construct, and which Maxine seemed to have carried almost halfway across the world lay crumpled, in ruins at their feet. 'Aren't you even going to read it?' she gasped, her eyes wide with unshed tears as she scrambled down and began picking the pieces of it up. 'You can't blame Mrs Martin for what's happened!'

To her complete astonishment he said, 'I have already spoken to your mother over the telephone and she told me you were on your way here. As for blaming her for what happened, I might not go as far as that, but I can find fault with any mother who brings up her son to believe he can have anything which takes his fancy, regardless of the pain this might inflict on others.'

'Colin isn't usually. . . .'

Before she could get anything more out, Maxine felt his hand on the back of her neck, hauling her to her feet again. 'Leave that,' and he took the remnants of the letter from her, thrusting them into a deep pocket, his eyes glinting with anger as he anticipated her defence of a man who had wronged him.

She felt his knuckles hard against her skin, his breath harsh on her face as he shook her like a dog. His hands hurt and only tightened when she tried to shake them off. They also seemed to burn where they touched, as his eyes had done when he first saw her. When he let her go she reeled and again grasped the carved piece of furniture for support.

Above her his face loomed, dark and menacing. 'Remember, Miss Martin, I won't listen when you speak of your brother. His name won't be mentioned in the house.'

'I'm sorry,' Maxine gasped breathlessly, panic showing in her eyes as she backed away from his cold, masculine anger. However was she going to extricate herself from this situation, which was none of her making? Somehow she couldn't think she owed Mrs Martin that much, but even so the words which might have explained her own innocence refused to come out.

Instead she heard herself murmuring weakly, 'Naturally, *monsieur*, you love your fiancée very much, and feel bitter against all the Martin family, but Mrs Martin is most upset.'

'I can well imagine.' His voice was cynical and the corners of his sensuous mouth curled. 'Undoubtedly she is as unhappy as you are that her precious son should defect, but I suspect her biggest worry concerns her business interests which, as you will know, I control. Otherwise she wouldn't have sent you.'

'You—you are mistaken, *monsieur*,' Maxine hesitated just a moment too long.

'Did she intend you should try and console me, *mademoiselle*?' Ignoring her feeble protest, he looked over her so insolently she squirmed. 'You may look like an angel, *mademoiselle*, and indeed your looks begin to intrigue me, but I know your reputation rather too well to believe you are one. Long ago your innocence was taken, and I am not to be impressed with second-hand goods.'

'How dare you!' Maxine spluttered, forgetting how any man in his position would be angry, and that she was here to placate.

'Please, *mademoiselle*,' suddenly he sounded weary, 'you don't have to pretend. I am not about to pronounce judgment and throw you to the jackals. Nor am I about to attack your so-called virtue. Right now, I am more interested in my dinner.'

Deep colour stained Maxine's pale cheeks as she sustained his taunting gaze. Knowing so little about Mrs Martin's daughter made it difficult to deny what this man implied about her. All she knew was that she had run off with a Mexican and, although Mrs Martin insisted they were, Colin had once told her his sister wasn't married.

Swallowing a sick rush of revulsion, because of her own stupidity, she whispered blankly, 'I think ...'

'Yes, *mademoiselle*?' At the point of turning away, Kurt d'Estier paused. 'What is it you think, this time?'

'Nothing, *monsieur*.' Helplessly she swallowed again, her head swimming as his dark glance held her captive. 'I was only going to say you must be feeling distressed, but I think I've already said that.'

'Distressed?' His eyes glittered with savage derision and once more his hand came out to grasp hold of her. 'You have a quaint turn of speech, which I don't seem to remember. You are beginning to arouse my curiosity, which might be good for a man of my low spirits.'

Maxine wondered how much he had loved the girl who had deserted him. Staring up at him, feeling his fingers biting her shoulders, she also wondered how his fiancée could have left a man like this in preference for Colin. She saw his powerful, lithe figure, his handsome head, the glint of self-assurance in his eyes and shivered. Perhaps she knew ...? Kurt d'Estier might not allow a girl even her own thoughts, never mind anything else! He would dominate, subdue, demand implicit obedience until his victim was utterly helpless, then he would take everything he wished without a twinge of conscience. She could feel it in the pressure of his hands. They communicated this frightening intelligence, as though he had spoken of it aloud.

Suddenly she was nervous of him, here in the great hall which held only the two of them. Because of the dim lighting their shadows were elongated, appearing to merge together and blend with the darker ones about them. The silence was complete, yet it seemed to whisper, to murmur in a language she didn't understand. It could have been the wind, or a heartbeat, the fluttering of a pulse. It could have been the quiver of tremulous lips longing to be soothed against a sensuous, seeking mouth.

Aware that she was staring, and fearful that such

hitherto unknown thoughts might be reflected in her
eyes, she jerked away. His hands fell from her shoulders,
releasing some of the strange tension which had held her
immobile. With a great effort she achieved cool form-
ality.

'I'm sorry to have intruded on your grief, *monsieur*,
but it was at your own request that I came here. I was
only told to give you this letter in Casablanca, then return straight home.'

'You won't be going home. Not straight away.' He was
nearer again and so immediately threatening she shrank
back.

'What do you mean?' Maxine felt a tremor run
through her. 'I realise I might not be able to go tonight,
but tomorrow . . . ?'

'There is the old saying, is there not, that tomorrow
never comes,' he smiled mirthlessly. 'No, *mademoiselle*,
for better or worse you stay here with me. Your mother
sent you.'

'Yes,' Maxine broke in, fear making her voice tremble.
She would have to explain about Mrs Martin. 'But you're
mistaken about. . . .'

'I would never be mistaken about that woman,' in turn
he interrupted grimly. 'Do you think I believe she would
send her only daughter all the way here just to deliver
a letter? Peace-offering would be nearer the mark. She
will hope I'll find it possible to console myself with you,
until your dear brother and my fiancée return. Don't
tell me you were not aware of this, *mademoiselle*?'

'It's not true,' Maxine whispered, aghast.

As if she hadn't protested, he went on, 'She remem-
bers, no doubt, that I was attracted to you when I first
saw you. At first sight I confess I was struck by your
beauty, but on looking closer I saw marks of dissipation
which made me wary. Yet you were so young I doubted
for once my own judgment. A few short enquiries, however, and what did I find out?'

While infuriated at his arrogance, that he should throw scorn on any girl for things he was probably just as guilty of himself, Maxine could only feel a horrified curiosity. 'What did you?' she asked.

'Nothing that should surprise you,' he sneered. 'From your brother himself I learnt how these so pale locks of yours are dyed,' his hand lifted to touch her hair, disparagingly, 'and I learnt also, though not from the same source, that even so young, you had taken lovers. You had, in fact, before you came with your mother to Casablanca, just returned from spending a holiday with a man old enough to be your father.'

When Maxine swayed and went white, he proceeded remorselessly, 'You don't have to pretend to be shocked, *mademoiselle*. That week you spent in Casa, when I held you in my arms it was for my own amusement, but even you were aware, when I kissed you, there was no spark between us. Maybe you were disappointed I went no further than a casual salute, but I'm afraid my interest disappeared. I don't think you have more than very occasionally crossed my mind, Miss Martin, not until these last two days.'

'If you would listen....' Maxine began desperately.

'Spare me,' he drawled. 'I'm not looking for excuses. But, *mon dieu*,' his eyes bored into her as his hand tilted her chin, 'I might, in the deplorable absence of my fiancée, be willing to be diverted by a woman who grows younger, rather than older. It makes one almost believe that self-indulgence can be no bad thing?'

'Please—stop!'

His mouth merely hardened; he had no intention of doing any such thing. The edges of his lips curled in pleasurable derision. 'If we do not hear from your brother, Miss Martin, and you are forced to search in the desert with me, your golden hair might be black again before you get back to civilisation.'

'You can't make me stay!'

'Until your brother returns my fiancée.' Kurt d'Estier was implacable.

Maxine's grey eyes widened, as for a moment she forgot her own predicament. 'I find it hard to believe you would really want her back, after this.'

Something about her eyes brought a frown to his face. He answered absently, 'Don't you believe, then, that true love should be capable of forgiving anything?'

Wordlessly she continued staring at him. She couldn't speak from experience as she had never been in love, but she had read a great deal. 'I would have thought so,' she whispered at last, 'but I've read that men are rarely as forgiving as women. And, as you seem to set such store by virtue, I can't see you forgiving a girl who'd been unfaithful with another man.'

Meeting the black anger in his face, she realised she hadn't chosen her words wisely. In an unhappy attempt to rectify this, she blurted out, 'I do understand you must be very despondent about your fiancée, and I hope you'll find her, but for myself, I must return to London. You've enjoyed teasing me about staying here, but as you appear to dislike me intensely, I'm sure you'll really be glad to see the last of me.'

Unfeelingly he shrugged his wide shoulders. 'I can assure you again, *mademoiselle*, you are not going home.' He paused suavely. 'I find it difficult to comprehend why you do not wish to help me find your brother.'

Maxine made a little unconscious gesture with her slim white hands. 'You must know, *monsieur*, that as a complete stranger to this country, I wouldn't be much help in trying to find anyone.'

'Of this I'm not so sure, *mademoiselle*. Your brother must have some affection for you. If he were to learn that I held you captive here, might it not bring him to his senses?'

Rather wryly she smiled. 'I'm afraid the average English family is not that close, *monsieur*. I don't think many Englishmen would jeopardise their future happiness for the sake of a sister, or anyone else.'

'No matter,' he spoke so decisively, she started, her half smile fading swiftly. 'You will remain with me until they are found. If you are sensible, Miss Martin, you will try and console me a little.'

Restraint deserting her as nerves took over, Maxine cried, 'Now you're being stupid! You can't go around acting like some desert sheik, because it just won't wash with me!'

'But this is exactly what I am, Miss Martin.'

'You can't be—not possibly . . .!'

'Ah, but I am!' His dark eyes pierced her cruelly, as though he enjoyed her apprehension. 'From my great-grandmother, whose blood I have in my veins, I have, by a devious twist of fate, inherited such a title.'

Stilling a gasp of rising terror, because it wasn't difficult to see now that he might easily fit the role of a barbaric conqueror, she tried to speak calmly. 'I heard you'd done a lot for some of the desert tribes, that you're very generous with your money.'

'I didn't buy my way in if that is what you mean,' he said coldly. 'I help them as much as I can, as I consider they are my people. In return they give me their intense loyalty. We are all brothers, and there is not one who would help you to escape from me, however big the bribe.'

'But you're French!' Maxine exclaimed, her voice trembling.

'Mostly,' he smiled sardonically. 'I have also in my family tree, which goes back several hundred years, a Spanish ancestor and an English one, which probably makes me a bit of a mongrel. This, however, is my land, and here, *mademoiselle*, I live and will most certainly die.'

He was so wholly adamant, there could be nothing more to say. They stared at each other, two antagonists,

neither willing to give way. Maxine's eyes were held by
the intentness of Kurt d'Estier's. She had the odd sensation of floating, of drifting in the unfathomable depth of
some dark seas. A pulse began beating at the base of her
throat as a wave of fire started sweeping inexorably
through her. Unconsciously she swayed, and his hand
reached out to steady her, but his clasp on her bare arm
only seemed to fan the already leaping flames.

'Mademoiselle?'

His voice, suddenly thicker, with more accent than
she had noticed before, brought her to her senses. Frantically she jerked away from him, saying the first thing
to enter her head, which, because she was so confused,
had to be what they had just been talking about. As if
seeking to offer a reason for her inner agitation, she whispered, 'What do you intend doing to Colin and your
fiancée, when you do find them?'

He appraised her narrowly for a further moment before replying. 'I haven't considered this fully,' he said
grimly, a muscle in his strong jaw tightening. 'For your
brother, I'm afraid, the consequences will not be pleasant,
but you can rest assured, *mademoiselle*, that should I not
find them, my reprisals will be equally unpalatable.'

The next morning Maxine woke with the continuing
conviction that none of this could have actually happened. Last night, after that coldblooded observation,
Kurt d'Estier had said she was to dine with him, and he
would wait while she changed. When she had told him
she had no other clothes but what she was wearing, he
had immediately ordered her to return to her room and
put on a djellaba. When she had refused, the dark anger
with which she was rapidly becoming familiar had appeared on his face, and when she still stood her ground,
if with difficulty, he had outraged and horrified her by
picking her up bodily and carrying her upstairs. She
might have weighed no more than a child as he had

crushed her against his hard chest and strode lithely upstairs with her, dumping her unceremoniously on her bed.

'You will change, *mademoiselle*. I do not dine with women dressed as you are.'

Maxine might have boiled at his arrogance if she hadn't felt so frighteningly disorganised, and looking down at her dusty, dirt-streaked dress, she had been aware that Mrs Martin might have said the same thing. In other circumstances she might have buried her pride and gone downstairs dressed in a djellaba, and enjoyed the novelty of it. But as it was she had been glad of an excuse not to face Kurt d'Estier again that night. She had sat in her room, trying to eat the beautifully prepared meal Vega brought her, trying to stop her stomach turning upside down every time she thought of Kurt d'Estier.

Fear had at first dominated her thoughts, then a peculiar curiosity. Since coming to work for Mrs Martin she had seen several men who might have been called handsome, but none who caught the imagination as Kurt d'Estier did. She could well believe he was of Berber descent. There was a complete ruthlessness about him, stamped on the lines of his otherwise very westernised features, a hint of primitive cruelty which might speak of madness, should the lust for revenge take him. There was also more than a hint, in the sensuous curve of his hard mouth, as to what direction his revenge might take if circumstances drove him to carrying it out. He would be a man well versed in the art of delighting a woman, Maxine had no doubt, but he would know, too, how to put her through hell!

Hiding her hot face in her pillows, Maxine had shuddered at such thoughts which the good nuns would have deplored, and had hoped that in sleep she might forget him. Yet his barbaric, handsome face had haunted her dreams and several times during the night she had awoken with his dark image in front of her.

Because of her restless night she overslept and knew the morning must be well advanced when she woke. Her watch had stopped, but scarcely waiting to consult it she jumped out of bed, running to the window. The glass, she found, set in deep recesses of stone, didn't open, but through it she could see vast expanses of barren hillside with mountains beyond, nothing which might deny a terrible isolation.

As the events of the previous evening came sweeping back, she felt her face pale as she shuddered. What chance did she have of leaving this place until Kurt d'Estier allowed it? Too late she realised how mistaken Mrs Martin had been in imagining he could be relied on to act as other men did. Dismally, she wondered how Mrs Martin could have decided it was safe for her to come. It was obvious that despite their business dealings, she didn't know Kurt d'Estier well enough to suspect the dangers of such a mission.

Fighting with what she knew to be rising hysteria, Maxine tried to calm herself. She had no wish to be considered a cringing coward, and if Vega were to catch her sobbing she would probably report it at once to her master. If Kurt d'Estier had contempt for her now, what would his attitude be if he caught her in a state of collapse?

Yet for all her efforts to stiffen her pride it wasn't easy to face the day bravely. What it would hold for her she had no idea. Even the thought of it brought an instinctive shrinking. The first thing she must do, she decided, was to find Kurt d'Estier. Somehow she must persuade him to change his mind about keeping her here, if he hadn't already done so. Last night he had been tired and naturally bitter, ready to vent his despairing rage on anyone, especially a girl whom he had taken to be the sister of the man who had so wronged him.

This was something which worried Maxine desperately. How was she to extricate herself from the position she was in? Did she even dare to? If she were to insist he listened to the truth—as he had refused to do the night before—he might have no pity at all on Colin, or on Mrs Martin, when he found the runaway pair. It couldn't do any harm, she supposed, to let him go on thinking she was Colin's sister, for another day or two. It was easy to see he had despised Colin's real sister, so Maxine didn't think he would do more than threaten with words. A man like that would only force his attentions on a girl if he was going to derive some pleasure from it, and his contempt for Mrs Martin's daughter seemed such that Maxine doubted he would even consider touching her!

Now she must get dressed and ask him to release her. If he refused again, then she must tell him in no uncertain manner that she was going! If this didn't work then she must try to get in touch with Mrs Martin. Kurt d'Estier would be going off to the desert again, to continue his search, which would give her the opportunity. The castle was isolated, but he must have some means of keeping in touch with the outside world. A business empire such as his wasn't run by remote control. He must be in almost constant contact, in spite of his liking for assuming the role of a wild desert sheik!

As she hadn't brought anything with her, Maxine had been forced to sleep in the brief silken nightdress which Vega had laid out. Glancing down at the transparent folds of it in dismay, she began looking for her own things, so she might get dressed. She was just beginning to realise they had gone when Vega appeared.

To Maxine's rather heated query, she replied with innocent politeness. 'The master took them, *mademoiselle*. He commanded they should be burnt.'

'Burnt? Oh, no!'

'Yes, *mademoiselle*.' Vega's smile grew even sweeter as she contemplated such masculine authority. 'So now you must wear what Vega brings.'

While alarm and anger chased through Maxine's eyes, Vega showed her the plain white tunic and trousers she carried. As usual the material was fine and silky, but she realised if she wished to see Kurt d'Estier before he went out, she must hurry. There was no time to give vent to her anger, and in any case she had no right to make Vega suffer. She must see it was Kurt d'Estier who did that!

'Very well,' she shrugged, her compliance in no way dispersing the fury in her heart as she held out her arms for the garments. 'But you can find my bra and panties?'

'Those, too, burnt,' Vega, with another happy smile, passed what Maxine could only describe as a mere scraps of lace. 'I have here new ones for you.'

Maxine stared in total disbelief at the man's effrontery, although she doubted that Kurt d'Estier had seen to the destruction of her clothing personally. She had offended him, last night, by refusing to change and dine with him. This would simply be his way of showing who was boss! As she had suspected, he was nothing but a savage and, for all she recognised the need for caution, she could hardly wait to get downstairs to tell him so.

Temper keeping her courage high, she washed quickly before dressing reluctantly in the garments she despised. Vega helped, tying the brief sash under Maxine's high, pointed breasts, exclaiming at the silkiness of her skin which showed between that and the top of the trousers. The trousers were full, but as she walked they displayed the long, slender length of Maxine's limbs. The material was caught in a tight band to the narrowness of her ankle, and her high, arched feet were thrust into fragile slippers with curved toes.

Unable to look at herself and impatient of Vega's low murmurings of admiration, she quickly brushed out her hair, then tied it back. It didn't look so glamorous as it did when hanging around her shoulders in waves, but the last thing she wanted was to look attractive to Kurt d'Estier. Besides, it was this totally unsuitable outfit which gave the false impression of beauty. It had nothing to do with the prim and proper girl inside it!

Ready, but far too conscious of her appearance, Maxine ran down the wide stairs. In her room she had drank the hot black coffee Vega brought her but hadn't been able to face the warm croissants and cherry jam. It had looked delicious and her healthy young appetite had clamoured to be satisfied. She had had to remind herself firmly that the food would probably still be there, after Kurt d'Estier had gone.

Rather to her surprise she caught sight of him immediately, crossing the great hall. Shaking back the light cloak which Vega had placed carefully around her shoulders, Maxine approached him courageously. He was obviously dressed to go out and her spirits lifted as she envisaged his departure.

As she approached he turned to stare at her, his eyes going over her swiftly, much as they had done on the previous evening. This time he lingered even more intently on certain aspects of her figure, which the open front of the cloak exposed seductively.

Hiding a fleeting disgust, at what she regarded as blatant sensuality, Maxine, her cheeks glowing pink, hastily dragged the folds of the caftan back around her. 'Monsieur,' she began, dispensing with the more usual greeting, but deciding not to risk antagonising him by betraying indignation, or complaining about her clothes, 'I must speak to you.'

'Indeed?' As she did, he ignored the formal 'good morning'. Nor did he appear unduly curious. He merely transferred his ironic glance from her person to her softly flushed face. His dark brows rose, as if the protectively fluttering movements of her hands served to amuse him. That no such action of hers would deter him from doing what he wanted was easy to read on his harshly attractive features.

'Yes,' she had to take a deep breath but clung stubbornly to the firm line she had decided on, 'I wish to return to Marrakesh. Before you go would you please arrange for a driver to take me there. I will pay you for your trouble, of course.'

'Really, Miss Martin? What makes you think I have a driver available?'

She had a feeling he was laughing at her, and the temper she was struggling with rose. She only suppressed it with difficulty. 'The man who brought me here last night must still be around. I insist you fetch him for me, as I'm certainly going.'

'But not to Marrakesh.' His eyes hardened as her defiance obviously displeased him. Not apparently willing to be soft with her any longer, he said curtly, 'You are coming to the desert with me.'

'No!' Startled, she forgot to hide her anger, as she glared up at him. 'No, I most certainly am not! You might force me to wear your ridiculous clothes, *monsieur*, but you can't make me go there. In fact,' she drew herself up to her full height, even though he still dwarfed her, 'you can't make me do anything I don't want to, can you, *monsieur*! I feel sorry for you, and offer my sympathy, but further than that I won't go.'

'Ah, but yes, my little spitfire, you will!' He came nearer, so Maxine could see the white glint of his cruel smile. 'I have it in my heart this morning, *mademoiselle*, to subdue someone. Why not you? It might make me feel somewhat better about your despicable family if I can make one of them suffer, even if it is only a little discomfort.'

Beating back a searing fright, Maxine retorted, 'I have the impression you don't like me, *monsieur*.'

'So?' His brows lifted.

'So it won't be exactly pleasurable to have to put up with my company, will it? You might find it's not worth the satisfaction you anticipate.'

He shrugged, making her immediately aware of his shoulders, their breadth and strength. 'I don't have any great expectations. You will simply be functional—to satisfy my lust, shall we say, if I begin suffering from frustration. Or to enjoy the frustration of yours, perhaps, when I don't feel like touching you.'

'How dare you!' Rage and fright warred with disgust for supremacy as she backed away from him. 'I refuse to go with you. No wonder your fiancée left you!'

His face went so cold she thought for a moment he was going to strike her, but suddenly he turned away to clap his hands. When, like faithful shadows, Izaak and Vega appeared, he spoke to them sharply in a language Maxine failed to understand.

Looking around wildly, in the hope of finding some means of evading his fury, and whatever diabolical plan he had in mind, she realised it would be impossible to escape. Before she got five yards he would be upon her. Like the prowling panther, his lithe body was made for speed as well as power. If she did get as far as the door, she guessed there would be men stationed outside.

Vega, obeying orders, brought a burnous which Kurt d'Estier, returning to Maxine's side, dropped indifferently over her shoulders. 'This will keep out the heat, as well as the cold. Come, say your farewells. We must be on our way.'

Ignoring these brusque instructions, feeling nothing but contempt for the pleading sweetness on Vega's face, Maxine threw the burnous to the ground, crying defiantly, 'I won't allow myself to be kidnapped! You can go and take a jump, monsieur, into the nearest—er—oasis!'

'Tiens!' he exclaimed, harshly, his eyes black as he grabbed her arm. 'Kidnapped? Who would believe you didn't come willingly to the desert with me, to search for your beloved brother?'

He moved to touch her and she backed away. What should she do now? As always, when reminded of what she owed Mrs Martin, she hesitated to expose the duplicity which Kurt d'Estier apparently already suspected. Could Maxine, no matter how desperate the present situation, make things worse for her? And, as she kept on telling herself, while Kurt d'Estier might enjoy frightening her, he could have no real intention of carrying out his absurd threats.

As she hesitated, shrinking from him like a small, defensive cat, he stunned her completely by calmly bending down and picking her up. She tried to speak, but articulation was impossible because of the fear that clutched her throat. Fright even robbed her of clear thought as he lifted her as easily as he had done the night before and carried her outside, to where a large truck stood waiting.

A man was sitting in the driver's seat, small and dark, extremely fierce-looking. Without a word, Kurt d'Estier almost threw Maxine in beside him, then climbed in after her himself.

His long, powerful arm forced her back against the leather as he slammed the door, while giving the driver instructions to leave. His voice was clipped, still taut with anger, which aroused in Maxine uncivilised reactions such as she had never known before.

Behind them two more vehicles, laden with men, started up, and as Kurt d'Estier signalled abruptly for them to follow, Maxine bent her fair head, sinking her small white teeth into the bared wrist of the arm he held across her.

Blood appeared, causing her to jerk back in horror, but not before she had seen the deep marks she had made on the hard sinew and flesh. Then the silence was ripped by Kurt d'Estier's muttered oath, his anger expressed through the ruthlessness of his hand on her head. As the grip of his hand tightened to twist her face towards him, half dazed with revulsion at what she had done, she shrank from the vicious rage in the gaze which he turned on her.

CHAPTER THREE

KURT D'ESTIER swore in French, very softly, yet the quiet tones on his voice held more menace than Maxine had ever dreamed of. The driver's attention had been drawn from the road, and as his startled glance fell on his master's bleeding wrist he exclaimed in alarm.

Breathing fire, Kurt d'Estier told him to look where he was going and the man reluctantly steadied the lurching vehicle again.

'You will suffer for this, *mademoiselle*,' Kurt d'Estier snarled harshly. '*Mon dieu*, I will tame you, if it's the last thing I do!'

Feeling totally limp from an excess of drama, Maxine's face went white. 'I'm—I'm sorry, *monsieur*,' she stammered, 'but if you will act like a savage in bringing me here against my will, then you can't expect civilised behaviour.'

'It is not I who is acting like a savage,' releasing her hair from his painful grasp, he spoke icily.

'I—I—hate you!' she gasped, yet was unable to meet his eyes. 'All the same, I didn't intentionally bite you.'

'I only wish to hear a sincere apology,' he countered acidly. '*Tiens*,' he drew forth a clean handkerchief from his pocket, 'you sound as though you suspect my blood might poison you!'

'I'm sorry,' she repeated, quite truthfully this time, yet not because she had hurt him, but rather that she seemed by such a childish action to have lost what little dignity she had possessed.

'Can I tie that for you?' she asked reluctantly, as he fumbled with the makeshift bandage. Relief that his quick anger appeared to be fading made her offer impulsively.

'You may.' Grimly he held out his wrist, as if he envisaged having it bitten again. 'And before you accuse me of making a great fuss over nothing, let me tell you, *mademoiselle*, that the slightest cut left unattended, in this country, can go septic very quickly in the heat.'

'I see.' Maxine's fingers trembled slightly, as she considered what this could mean.

'Do not be so remorseful, Miss Martin,' he taunted. 'Just behave yourself for a while, that is all I ask. My driver will have a long enough tale to tell without adding more to his story. If you had been his woman, he would have taken you and beaten you until you begged for mercy.'

'Then perhaps you should explain that I am not your woman.' She tried to speak evenly, reminding herself that she might be better to leave well alone and be grateful to have got off so lightly.

'Ah, but he does not know that,' Kurt d'Estier drawled coolly. 'They will simply assume, these people, that because I bring you to the desert you belong to me. I'm afraid what little face I have lost through not immediately chastising you must be made up. It will amuse me to pass the next few hours in deciding exactly how I will bring this about.'

Maxine's fingers jerked nervously on the bandaged wrist as she let it go. Again she had to remember not to take everything this man said too seriously. Wrenching her eyes from his coldly impassive face, she gazed through the window, noticing that the countryside they were travelling through so swiftly was still dry and barren.

'Where exactly are we going, *monsieur?*' she asked stiffly.

'The desert,' he replied, so that she was none the wiser. 'We travel by car as far as we can, then use horses. If I used names it would only confuse you.'

'In other words,' Maxine said sullenly, 'you don't want me to know?'

'It is of little consequence.' He sounded bored. 'My movements are never that mysterious. Morocco is a richly diverse country, *mademoiselle*, her secrets not easily learnt. I can certainly name the various territories as we come to them, but we won't be entering any of the major towns.'

Sitting as far away from him as possible, Maxine tried to think of something else, but it wasn't easy, with her stomach sick with apprehension, to pretend she was just making a normal journey. They didn't stop for lunch. Kurt d'Estier simply passed her a canteen of water and some sandwiches of rough rye bread, which he also shared with his driver. After this, drowsy with the heat, Maxine drooped in her seat, then slept. Hours later she woke with a start to realise they had stopped.

'Come, *mademoiselle*!' Kurt d'Estier was shaking her gently. She must have slumped against him and was lying practically in his arms. The cloak had come open at the front, revealing the transparent djellaba she wore underneath. His eyes were on the shadowed hollow between her seductive breasts. How long, she wondered, her face scarlet with heated resentment, had he been looking at her thus?

Drawing her slim body quickly away from him, she exclaimed angrily, 'Why didn't you wake me sooner, *monsieur?*'

'No hurry,' he drawled, reading her thoughts mockingly. 'You slept like a baby. For once I enjoyed having you near me, so suppliant for the shelter of my hated arms that I could have held you for ever.'

Mortified, she scrambled from the truck, aware again of a peculiar excitement running through her. Expecting they had reached the end of their journey, at least for that day, she thought to see people, and a small village, or casbah. Instead there was only a group of stamping horses. 'Where do we go now?' She turned to Kurt d'Estier sharply, her sleepiness fading rapidly.

'Do you ride, *mademoiselle*?' His voice was suave but unconcerned as to whether she did or not, and he made no attempt to answer her question.

Without stopping to wonder if Colin's real sister rode or not, she shook her head. 'No. I would only hold you back, *monsieur*. If you intend putting me on a horse, especially in this ridiculous outfit I'm wearing, I would only fall off.'

A frown creased his broad brow. 'As you wish, girl. If you choose to ride with me at least you cannot escape, and my horse can easily carry two.'

Stubbornly, terror rising again, Maxine stood her ground. 'I refuse to go any further, *monsieur*. You're nothing but a common criminal, a despicable tyrant!'

'Your language is too strong,' he retorted harshly, his eyes darkening, the conversation clearly beginning to bore him. 'Who would believe you didn't willingly join in the search for your brother? How many times must I repeat this before I convince you?'

One glimpse at the huge stallion which a Berber was leading forward assured Maxine that Kurt d'Estier was not indulging in idle threats. Wholly alarmed, she turned, running wildly away from him.

Before she had got more than a few yards he caught her. Cursing under his breath, while she struggled fiercely, he threw her up on to the high-pommelled saddle, mounting swiftly behind her. Thrusting his feet into the broad stirrups, he issued a sharp command to the poker-faced men about him, then moved off.

If he imagined this conceded him victory, he would

soon find out his mistake! Maxine went on struggling, determined to give him so much trouble that he would be glad to change his mind about taking her. There was something else she was fighting, too, but it was too complex for her to understand. She didn't care for the feelings Kurt d'Estier aroused in her, but what they were exactly she couldn't tell. The strange kind of tension which sprang up between them when they looked at each other was better ignored. Her hands clenched to fists, she hit out at him until he imprisoned them both by grasping her wrists.

'*Mademoiselle*,' he rasped, 'you may wish it were so, but I don't have unending patience. Unless you want to be held so close, learn to behave yourself.'

'Never!' she gasped, her dry lips muffled against him. Goaded beyond measure, she continued, 'I don't know how—considering what Colin has done, you can bear to have me near you!'

He laughed tauntingly, still holding her hands. 'Somehow I am losing all sense of having known you, Miss Martin. It is as if you were a stranger, yet not a stranger.'

He was enigmatic. 'A stranger?' she faltered, seeing all her efforts laid in ruins.

'Yes, *mademoiselle*. It is crazy, is it not, that you are getting between me and other, far more important things I have to do? When I look at you, it is as if it were for the first time.' His voice grated with self-mockery. 'Perhaps if I can tame you, my small, spitting cat, you will teach me the secret of eternal youth. I am only thirty-five, yet sometimes I feel my own youth is fading.'

'I have no secrets,' she choked, forgetting the one she hadn't told him, which would have immediately explained that which puzzled him. 'You talk foolishly. Would you be sensible for a moment and put me down!'

As she wriggled unsuccessfully, the saddle and his tightening arms bruised her. She felt his heart thudding heavily against her and the uneven response of her own.

Against her slender thighs she felt the pressure of his hard leg, and as though the movements of her soft body provoked him against his will, his muscles tensed. Feeling an answering heat rush through her, she tried to draw away from him, but he merely crushed her closer.

His hand freed her wrists so his fingers might slide to her throat, under her chin. Turning her face up to him, he said, 'Once you almost begged me to hold you thus. I am only obliging, even if I am ten years late. Perhaps we should make up for lost time?'

She made a faint sound which was like a dry sob in her throat, an unconscious plea for mercy, but he bent his dark head, taking her defenceless mouth with his in a kiss of such ferocity that it removed all her breath. The world spun and everything in it, and high up on the huge horse she might well have been floating. His mouth burnt as he forced her slender neck backwards, and under her blouse his searching hand found her heaving breast. When he let her go and she opened dazed eyes, and his face swam with the sun above her.

'I hate you!' she whispered, when she could find sufficient strength to wrench her eyes from his smouldering gaze. 'Hate you!' she repeated, striving desperately to believe it.

His hands left her to control the prancing horse, to urge him to more speed. As the animal broke into a swift canter, he muttered indifferently, 'I can enjoy a woman, *mademoiselle*, without having her love me. I told you this morning that you would suffer. Maybe the knowledge that my threat was no idle one will be sufficient to still that regrettable tongue of yours and enable us to get on with our journey.'

It was almost dark when they stopped the next time. Night came, Maxine had discovered, with an almost alarming suddenness in this land, but this evening a faint glimmer of daylight seemed to linger as if, she thought derisively, even the elements sought favour with the man

who held her so intolerantly before him. His men—
Maxine had counted about a dozen—had ridden slightly
behind him, but she didn't know whether this was a
mark of his rank or simply the age-old tendency to
follow a natural leader. She had learnt, even in so short
a time, that Kurt d'Estier, with his tall, broad-shouldered
figure was a man who commanded respect. His men, if
that was what they were, these Berbers of the desert,
called him Sidi, and always with deference.

When Kurt d'Estier threw up his arm in a signal to
halt they were in the shelter of a small grove of palm
trees. As he steadied the great stallion so she might slide
to the ground, Maxine glanced uncertainly about her.
Her limbs felt strangely weak, forcing her to stand still
a moment until the strength flowed back into them. It
had been easy enough sitting on the horse, held there by
her captor's strong arms, but the effect of being near to
him for so long was something she hadn't bargained for.

'Are you all right, *mademoiselle?*' The harshness of
his voice took away any illusion of concern, and she
nodded silently, without looking at him.

Very quickly she had realised she would just be wasting her breath if she continued with a verbal battle, and
that to fight him in any other way was impossible in
their present position. A dozen times the urge to tell him
who she really was crossed her mind, but indecision
plagued her. Besides, when she had once tried to tell him,
hadn't he merely laughed, and she doubted if there was
any real danger of him molesting her in any way, especially when he obviously expected to find his fiancée at
any moment. What sort of woman must his fiancée be,
she found herself wondering, to have captured the affec-
tions of two such men? Men like Kurt d'Estier and Colin
Martin.

Gazing around the waste of sand, made even more
desolate by a rising wind which made lonely noises in
the treetops, she wondered fleetingly where Colin could

be hiding in such a wilderness. He had never struck her as being a very adventurous kind of person. She could imagine him taking a girl he fancied to some luxurious hotel, or a flat in a city or famous resort, but never here where there was only empty space and silence. All Maxine had seen during the hours in which they had crossed the desert was a drift of sand. A distant sand-storm, Kurt d'Estier had told her grimly, when he had seen her looking, but mercifully it wasn't coming their way. This, apart from a lone vulture, had been all that had caught her eye. Now, as the stars came out, with a brilliance which might have rivalled the moon in other lands, she saw how the men were replenishing the fire they had lit, on which to cook the evening meal.

One of the rugged bronzed men brought Maxine a small bowl of water. 'It is all there is to spare.' Kurt d'Estier bore down on her, on silent feet, out of the darkness. 'This is an oasis, but it has dried up, so we must be stringent with our supplies until we reach camp tomorrow.'

'I wasn't complaining, *monsieur*.'

He nodded, leaving her to get on with her ablutions. There was no privacy as no tent had been erected for her, but she wasn't unduly disturbed by the lack of even the basic amenities. Another time she might have en-joyed it, for she was young, with a latent thirst for ad-venture occasionally warming her blood. As she watched the black silhouettes of the Berbers outlined against the leaping flames, her nostrils tantalised by the smell of cooking food, she felt an odd flicker of excitement deep within her, a sense of yearning anticipation she couldn't account for. When the tremor of warning came she was grateful and began industriously to wash her face.

After drying herself as best as she could on her clean handkerchief, she combed her hair, then tied it back again. The air was cooler and after she finished she put the bowl to one side and sat down on the thick burnous she had been wearing.

Kurt d'Estier brought her dinner himself, and she ate the plain but plentiful fare ravenously.

'One only learns to appreciate food when away from the civilisation of the city, *mademoiselle.*'

Selfconsciously she flushed, aware that she had been practically gobbling. 'You forget I've had very little to eat all day,' she said defensively. She wondered why he called her Mademoiselle so frequently. Recalling his stated opinion of Mrs Martin's real daughter, Mademoiselle sounded somehow too young and naïve for that particular lady.

He smiled sardonically, without much humour. 'I don't criticise your appreciation of good food. I only hope you have the same appetite for—other things.'

Again Maxine felt her cheeks grow hot. What he meant she wasn't really sure, but his words brought a thrill of fear. Staring across at him over the remains of their meal, she sought determinedly to alleviate her uneasiness by showing a little spirit. He still wore the white, corded haik he had worn all day. Curiously she wondered what he would look like without it. Her eyes lifting to it pointedly, she asked with impudent impulsiveness, 'Do you sleep in it, *monsieur*?'

'No, *mademoiselle*, I do not. As you may discover.'

Maxine gulped. The time his meaning was unmistakable. His face hardened and there was something very like a threat in his voice. Suddenly she wished he was not so tall and intimidating, that he would stop acting like a lordly pagan! It didn't help that the demeanour of his men aided and abetted this impression. He was arrogant, steeped in pride, but whatever happened he must never guess she was nervous of him.

'Threats,' she shrugged, staring at him defiantly, 'are easily uttered, *monsieur*. Carrying them out is another thing. England might seem a long way off, but I warn you, if anything should happen to me you would have to face severe reprisals.'

His eyes, glinting with mockery, proved another humiliation. 'Should this scare me, my little butterfly?'

If she hadn't eaten every scrap of her dinner, she would have thrown it at him! As it was she could only fling defiance and hope the hate he must read in her eyes might deflate his outsize ego.

'You may be amused, *monsieur*,' she spat, 'but it is I who might get the last laugh! You forget I'm not used to the desert. If I should collapse and the authorities hear of it, what then? And, if I were taken ill, what use would I be in helping you in your search for your fiancée?'

'Do not occupy yourself, *mademoiselle*, with constant thoughts of reprisal. You waste both your time and mine.' Forbiddingly he rose. 'I have lived too long in this country, *ma chérie*, to pay much attention to the rantings of women. They are merely chattels—with their uses.'

Maxine almost choked over her coffee. 'Indeed, *monsieur*! Now I begin to understand why your fiancée left you.'

His sudden anger was frightening, if it did only momentarily show on his face. Maxine's arm was taken in a grip which was meant to hurt as his glance flamed down on her. 'You are impertinent, Miss Martin. I'm warning you, for your own good, I won't take much more.'

He didn't need to be more explicit, the glinting fury in his eyes said it for him. 'Come,' he relented slightly, as her face paled, 'you must sleep. Perhaps a good rest might help to still this sharp tongue, which I don't seem to remember. I don't remember, either, that you were so addicted to calling me *monsieur*?'

With this enigmatical comment he led her away from the fire to where two rugs were spread beside a pile of saddles on the sand. 'I'm afraid you will have to put up with my company,' he said.

They were some distance from the men, but she looked at him coldly. 'I'd rather be on my own.'

He took no notice but pointed to the ground as he picked up another rug. 'Lie down,' he ordered, as though she hadn't spoken, 'and put this over you. I can protect, you foolish girl, as well as other things.'

This, reminding Maxine of dangers she could not be unaware of, forced her to comply, even while she glared up at him.

Mockingly he dropped the rug over her tense body. 'I'm glad you are willing to see reason.'

The stars were huge and bright above her head, but she turned, burying her face in her makeshift pillow, not wishing to see the stars, to be entranced by them and the magic of the night. There was a kind of erotic affinity between those stars and those who slumbered beneath them in the desert. In spite of her despair and indignation Maxine couldn't help being conscious of it. A natural response to something sensuous in the atmosphere permeated her whole being. It was a reaction which had something primitive about it, and from which she shrank. Repelled yet fascinated, she felt like some small creature being lured to its doom. It was making her recall vividly how it had been when Kurt d'Estier had kissed her. It made her long, with a curious restlessness, for something she had never known.

Kurt d'Estier lay on his back beside her. She heard his impatient sigh replaced by another of temporary contentment as he stretched and relaxed after the rigours of the day. Restlessly he turned, making no attempt to touch her, yet it was listening to his movements, as each small sound was emphasised by the silence of the night, which eventually sent her to sleep.

Amazingly she slept soundly, awakening to find him leaning over her, propped on his elbow, studying her intently. Her hair, loosened from its tie, was spread over her pillow, the silvery gold of it glinting in the rising sun. Her face, faintly flushed from the sweetness of her sleep under the stars, was smooth and unblemished.

As she opened her violet-grey eyes to find his face only a few inches from her own, her first feelings of contentment faded to fright. '*Monsieur!*' she gasped, a rush of panic pressing her back against the rugs on which she lay. She saw suddenly that he wasn't wearing his headdress, that he had thick, dark hair with a slight wave to it—a wave which he mightn't control as easily as he did everything else. He was, she recognised, with a quickening of pulse, an extremely good-looking man. His face might be rugged and strong but, for her, it might also be unforgettable. 'Please,' she whispered, unsure as to whether she was reproving her traitorous senses or the man who was regarding her so closely. How long had he been studying her thus?

'Don't be disturbed,' he said dryly, the contempt in his voice making her cheeks grow hot. 'When I wish to make love to you I will choose a more private place. I merely had a curiosity to see the colour of your eyes in the first light, and no light can reveal the truth more clearly than that of the desert.'

'My eyes?' Wholly disturbed by what he had just said to her, Maxine's thoughts whirled in confusion.

'I have rarely seen eyes more beautiful, *mademoiselle*. The grey is particularly memorable. It is making me wonder how I could forget.'

Goaded by a tremor, which she refused to believe was jealousy, she murmured, 'Other eyes must have intrigued you since then, *monsieur*?'

As he continued to stare at her, he shook his head. His own eyes she had taken to be black, but she saw now they were really an extremely dark blue. It was only when his emotions were moved, and he was angry, that they took on the hue of this other colour.

A hint of recklessness drove her to taunt him, 'Don't tell me you deny this, Kurt d'Estier!'

Anger rewarded her persistence. His mouth hardened

and his hand went out to grasp a handful of golden hair. As if to punish her, he jeered, 'Your eyes are a beautiful soft grey, *mademoiselle*. In Morocco we have every colour but that. They remind me of the rain which seldom comes. Your skin is pink and white, your hair like a cloud of gold and your mouth resembles the petals of a rose. The desirability of your body has let me sleep only uneasily through the night. Does that satisfy your insatiable appetite for flattery, which leads you to dance so beguilingly from one man to another?'

The blow he struck might have been physical as she jerked upright. The melting response which he had referred to, that had unconsciously softened her eyes, faded to anger. Wildly she struck out at him with the one weapon she possessed, that which she had used with such good effect the night before. 'It's not difficult to see why you couldn't keep your fiancée, *monsieur*. A woman needs love and tenderness, as much as strength, and you only offer unfeeling brutality.'

To match hers and surpass it, his anger mounted. 'I've warned you already, I won't tolerate your impertinence. When the time comes that you have to pay for it, don't complain. *Dieu!*' his dark eyes bored into hers as he removed his hand from her hair, 'I don't know why I bother to lose my temper with you! You remind me of a spoilt child, with your constant lashing out. Sometimes I find it difficult to believe you are far from being one.'

Maxine shivered, as if all the warmth had gone from the sun. Fearfully she gazed at him, her soft mouth trembling. Unconsciously provocative, she moistened dry lips.

'By the saints,' he growled threateningly, under his breath, his eyes fixed on her face, 'I am almost looking forward to taming you, *mademoiselle*. A long time ago you should have had a master. Perhaps I was a fool to reject you all those years ago, but I'm not likely to repeat such a mistake. In fact, looking at you now, I might not find it difficult to believe I am your first lover. Apart from a technical point or two, of course.'

Managing to speak, with supreme effort, Maxine cried, 'You can't let revenge drive you as far as that, surely?'

'Why not?' he asked insolently. 'Maybe we can comfort each other. You have a strangely lost look about you, for all your infamous reputation.'

Feeling coldly helpless, Maxine stared down at her hands, anywhere to escape that harshly unfeeling face. 'If you would leave,' she muttered, her voice low, 'I would like to tidy myself before you force me to continue this senseless journey.'

'Most certainly.' He rose abruptly, but his tones were far from apologetic as he conceded her request. With a mocking bend of his dark head he left her, striding towards his men who were already beginning to stir.

Wrenching her eyes from his tall figure, her glance was caught by the imprint of his body on the sand. He had scorned to use his rug, making do with only his thick burnous, and at times during the night he must have been very close as their two outlines appeared to merge. Again she shivered, hoping uneasily that she hadn't been the one to span the gap first. It had been there between them as she had fallen asleep, but if he hadn't slept, and he had all but confessed he hadn't, then it could only have been herself.

Later that day, after stopping just once to eat another frugal meal and water the horses, they came to the Berber encampment which Kurt d'Estier had spoken of. Having had to ride in front of him, held close to him, Maxine was relieved beyond measure that they appeared to have reached their destination. She felt she had had enough of his hard mockery, the long silences interspersed only by his sarcastic remarks, to last her a lifetime!

This was a larger oasis than that where they had

stopped the previous night. To her surprise she saw the encampment was strewn with low black tents and that there were women among the men who occupied them. To one tent, much larger than most of the others, Kurt d'Estier led her.

'We stay here for a few days,' he said curtly, 'so I'd advise you to accept this, *mademoiselle*. I have much work to do as well as business of my own to see to, so make yourself comfortable. Then,' he mocked, 'I shall not feel so guilty at having to deprive you of my constant company.'

For all she was so stiff and sore she could have cried, Maxine found herself gazing with a kind of awe around the tent he had brought her to. She had read how many of the desert tribes lived, but never had she imagined she would ever be asked to share their environment. Yet she couldn't think that this well appointed tent represented the general living standards of the average desert nomad.

Guessing something of what was going through her mind, Kurt d'Estier glanced at her coldly. 'You forget the tribes in this area at least look on me as their rightful leader and treat me accordingly. This tent is always available when I visit them.'

'Which can't be so often, surely?' She tried not to look at the woman who was spreading mats and putting down cushions. A welcome for their great lord and master and the woman he had brought with him, no doubt?

'Do not look so sceptical,' he thrust her further into the first room, a little away from the door and gestured for the woman to leave them. 'There are others of good authority who are always here. I do not pretend to run their lives, but I help in every other way possible.'

'With money, I suppose?'

His proud face darkened. 'Money—my money, *mademoiselle*—has done much for these people. More than I

might have achieved by being with them all the time.
The desert is a hard taskmaster. It is rarely willing to
support more than a few sheep and goats, which supply
food. A nomad very seldom has anything to sell in order
to obtain cash to buy the things which we consider a
necessary part of our everyday living. So do not be so
quick to heap scorn on men like myself.'

She shrugged, beating down a quick feeling of shame,
with a pretence of indifference. 'You can't expect me to
interest myself in that which I hope to leave as soon as
possible. As for gratitude, that's the last thing I could feel
towards you.'

'I should advise you not to do anything foolish,' he
said coldly. 'You will be allocated a servant and when
you bathe in comfort and eat at my table you might be
wise to remember that I am the provider.'

'I'd rather starve!'

His voice was silky. 'My answer to that should be to
imprison you in some inferior tent, of which we have
several, but in depriving you, *mademoiselle*, I would
also be depriving myself. So I will take no notice of your
childish rantings. I'll leave you, though, with a word of
warning. If you refuse to bath and change your clothing
I will personally see to it myself. My people would expect
me to suitably chastise a woman who defies me. If I did
not then I would certainly lose face.'

'Do they know the true reason why I'm here?' she
jeered.

He laughed in her face. 'They understand I have my
troubles and seek a woman to comfort me. No one will
lift a finger to help you.'

'Then I'll just have to help myself, won't I!'

His mouth curled, in the sneer she was getting too
familiar with. 'Somehow I can't see you doing that, *ma
chérie*, not with your usual expertise, anyway. I've no
doubt you've wriggled out of many uncomfortable situ-
ations by the skin of your charming white teeth, but fate

has a peculiar habit of catching up with little cheats, especially those who are too promiscuous for their own good.'

Taking an involuntary step backwards, she stared up at him. 'You sound both insulting and threatening, *monsieur*, but I don't know what you're talking about.'

'Yes, you do.' Snatching her arm, he dragged her close to his hard body, fixing her immobile with his relentless dark eyes. 'You are aware of a certain feeling between us, *mademoiselle*. As yet I am not quite sure what it is myself, but I intend passing a few intriguing hours finding out. And I don't mean to be denied that which you've squandered so generously in the past on other men.'

'I've told you, you're mistaken!' she cried, her face going white as his words filled her with dread. She knew he spoke the truth, there was something between them. When he looked at her, when he had kissed her there was the sensation of two live wires meeting and fusing, but whatever the cause it could only be an illusion. Nothing permanent could develop in so short a time. 'You're quite mistaken,' she repeated, tensely.

'I'm never mistaken, *mademoiselle*.'

'You have been about your fiancée!'

His eyes glittered, 'You can't leave that alone, can you? I won't tell you again!'

Her own temper rising hotly, she held his smouldering stare. 'I'm not that easily intimidated!'

'No, you're not, are you?' his anger changed quickly to a soft mockery, which she found even more frightening. 'You aren't the same girl who ran, almost screaming, when you thought a camel was going to bite you, and who declared hysterically that the heat of the sun was ruining your complexion? This new Maxine arouses my interest, and I have need of this interest—of the passion you move in me.'

Before she could reply he let her go abruptly and left the tent, leaving her trembling.

With a pounding heart, Maxine tried to steady herself, deploring the strange excitement which made her bones feel like water. Only a fool would ignore such danger as she was in. Kurt d'Estier was a man who might stir any woman's senses, and the remains of his love affairs must be scattered around many countries. He might pretend to be a desert sheik, but this would just be one of his many roles. She didn't really suppose it would make any difference to him to know she wasn't Mrs Martin's daughter, and it was simply going to be a waste of breath to continue trying to convince him.

A girl came in, one not unlike Vega, who said her name was Zara. She spoke no English and only a few words of French, so Maxine had some difficulty in making herself understood. Kurt d'Estier must have sent someone like this on purpose, so that Maxine wouldn't be able to question her or to enlist her aid in trying to escape. Zara brought water and while Maxine was glad to bath she insisted on managing herself. As Vega had done, Zara reluctantly contented herself with watching, and Maxine decided to let her stay. If nothing else, the girl could assure Kurt d'Estier that his prisoner was washed and clean. Which might just happen to put him in a kinder, more reasonable mood!

CHAPTER FOUR

DARKNESS fell as Maxine finished her bath and Zara rubbed delicately scented oils into her aching limbs. The girl, she had discovered, was surprisingly efficient and had the most soothing hands. There was still the difficulty of the language barrier, but Zara appeared to know what was needed without being told. The complicated gestures Maxine had envisaged were not necessary, and again she wondered at such expertise. It was a strange thing to find in the desert and a frown touched her smooth white brow. It made her realise how little one race of people might know about another, and she sighed regretfully as Zara escorted her back to the main room.

After Zara had gone, Maxine stood uncertainly, gazing about her. As before, a feeling of blind panic attacked her and she had to fight desperately to keep such terror under control. Sobs rose in her throat, and she had just managed to pull herself together when Kurt d'Estier joined her. It was a while since Zara had left her and she had been thinking hopefully that she might not be seeing him again that day. When he strode into the tent her eyes widened with a dismay she wasn't quick enough to hide. His mouth curled cynically when he saw it.

To Maxine it seemed incomprehensible that though she was filled with loathing the sight of him should accelerate her heartbeats. Anxiously she hoped he hadn't caught her swiftly indrawn breath. Wearing a white, silken tunic, open at the neck, with wide, baggy trousers similar to her own, he had the look of a handsome, dangerous animal. His head was bare, his dark hair freshly brushed, his skin and hands well cared for and clean. Despite the hardness of his day, he emanated a hard vitality, a relentlessness which made her shiver.

Bowing, with a mocking briefness, from the waist, he flicked a glance over her pale, uneasy young face, resting appreciatively on her long fair hair which she had left hanging loose as her head ached.

'You don't seem particularly pleased to see me,' he murmured, 'but I hope you are feeling better?' When she didn't answer, his eyebrow rose sardonically, 'At least I hope you're feeling well enough to join me for dinner?'

'Yes,' she agreed stiffly to this. But for all she stared at

him with apparent hostility, she thought twice of telling
him she would much rather have eaten alone. Already
her intuition was becoming quick in warning her when
she was treading on dangerous ground. To have to put
up with more of his company seemed too much to bear,
yet she managed a cool glance which disguised the worst
of her antipathy, while not betraying how conscious she
was of his disturbing masculinity.

He still stared at her closely, and she felt herself growing hot as his eyes roamed her slender body. He had
obviously no conscience about embarrassing her. It was
as if he considered he had bought and owned her. A
Frenchman, of course, might do this kind of thing easily,
considering it complimentary, and many women would
regard such attention as flattering. For Maxine her only
reaction was a desire to flee. She was not so much
flattered as frightened—if in a wholly unfamilar way.
She wished she had been wearing the woollen sweater
she had been wearing the day before she left England.
It was a pity that February in the desert was too hot for
wool. Yet in the gauzy outfit she had on now she felt
almost indecent. Defensively she crossed her arms in
front of her, not caring that her action brought a glitter
of fleeting amusement to Kurt d'Estier's insolent eyes.

The woman who brought their meal went out again.
As they sat down, he said derisively, 'You shrink in the
most virginal way when I look at you, ma chérie. How
is it you still retain such an air of innocence?'

'Perhaps because I am innocent, monsieur.'

Unpleasantly he laughed, 'Come, Miss Martin. Long
ago I stopped being that naïve!'

'You graduated to being insulting, monsieur, which
can't be an improvement.'

Again his firm mouth twisted. 'You're no novice when
it comes to insults yourself,' he observed her obstinate
little chin speculatively, 'You have spirit, ma chère, but
if we are to get to know each other better then you must

call me Kurt. You didn't used to find it so difficult.'

'So you keep on telling me, *monsieur*.'

'I wish to hear you say it. Now!' the softness of his voice didn't disguise his determination, as he stared at her resentfully flushed cheeks.

'Oh, don't be so silly!' Without complying she began deliberately to eat her dinner, yet the odd provocation of his demands took away the taste. In other circumstances she knew she would liked to have called him Kurt, but the dangers of such intimacy were too apparent for her to give way on this issue tonight. Once on a downhill trend, she might easily find herself tumbling headlong into the unknown. Better to stay with what was safe than to risk being carried beyond her depth by the experienced manipulating of a man like Kurt d'Estier.

He was evidently not used to being accused of being foolish. 'You forget yourself, *mademoiselle*.' His softer mood disappeared in coldness.

'And you forget your sense of humour,' she retorted scornfully.

'I might find that when I find my fiancée,' he surprised her by replying grimly. 'So if my temper doesn't please you, you have only yourself to blame—and your brother!'

For the next few minutes they ate in total silence. Then Maxine asked bitterly, 'While dwelling on your own troubles, do you ever spare a thought for other people's? Have you ever considered how Mrs Martin is going to worry when I don't return?'

'Why should I?'

'Because I can't believe anyone could be that selfish,' she cried. 'My God, you beat everything!'

'Take care, girl, I don't beat you!' he paused, as the same woman who had brought their dinner left them coffee. 'Men of the desert know how to settle a waspish tongue.'

'It's surely not a crime to speak one's mind?'

'Sometimes it is not very wise.'

Over the coffee cup he passed she met his bland stare
and would have liked to have flung the cup at him.
'Perhaps not,' she agreed, fear lending her caution. 'In
future I'll try to keep my opinions to myself, but this
doesn't mean I'll change them, or stop thinking them.'

Harshly he sighed, 'Your opinion of me doesn't have
to be verbally expressed, *chérie*, I can see it in your
eyes. It must be up to me to change it for you.'

Some music wafted through the open door of the
tent, and from somewhere in the camp came the high,
thin notes of a woman singing. The night air was
sensuously warm, the darkness bringing a gentle softness,
hiding the barrenness of the limitless sand dunes, the sight
of which could, on occasion, strike fear into even the
strongest. Already Maxine was discovering how the night
and dawn in the desert could hold a kind of magic, but
daylight, with temperatures seldom below a hundred,
could be a time of endurance.

She made no reply to his last comment but was aware
that his eyes never left her. He didn't appear to care
that he made her uncomfortable as he went on studying
her face and figure. It was clear to Maxine that he was
still puzzled as to why the years had changed her so
little, but by now she knew better than to waste breath
trying to explain.

After they finished their coffee he went to close the
flap on the tent door. The charcoal burner glowed red,
there was only one lamp and the tent was cosy. Quickly
Maxine rose, a feeling of nervousness returning which
removed all traces of her former bravado. 'If you will
excuse me, I'd like to retire for the night.'

'Why?'

'Because I'm tired,' she said, her eyes defying him to
make her stay.

His mouth twisted fractionally. 'You've done nothing
but sit in front of me all day, tantalising my senses, yet

you tell me you're tired! You don't expect me to believe it?'

A storm of alarm swept through her as he strode back to her, catching her in his arms, and because she had refused to believe it could happen, she felt too stunned to move. She flashed him a glance, her throat dry. 'Please, release me at once, monsieur!'

'No.' His face hardened as he stared down into her frightened eyes. 'I might later,' he said almost curtly, 'but something about you won't let me do it immediately. Just be still, *mademoiselle*, while I endeavour to satisfy my curiosity.'

She felt the jar of his gaze through her body, taking away her faint moan of protest as he lowered his head. His mouth seemed full of a harsh hunger as it caught hers and his arms slid right around her. Her lips, which instinctively she closed, were brutally assaulted, crushed until forced open under his.

She kept her eyes closed, her soft mouth burning, as though the shock waves from it were composed of flames. Insidious little flames, darted from his warm lips which left no part of her mouth unexplored. They rushed hither and thither, flicking to every inch of her helplessly yielding body. It was only when she began trembling really badly that he stopped.

Slowly his head came up, his eyes on her bruised, stinging mouth, studying the damage, the way in which she was visibly shaking. He said, a trifle thickly, 'All this, *mademoiselle*, and we have hardly yet got started. For one of your experience, I'm surprised.'

'You brute!' she found enough voice to whisper hoarsely. 'I'll make you pay for this if it's the last thing I do!'

'Shush!' As though he was calming a fractious young filly, he spoke softly, holding her to him when she would have pushed him away. His hand came out to move the heavy hair from off her hot face as he bent his lips to her shell-like ear. 'Maybe I am being a little too rough, *chérie*,' he kissed the side of her cheek gently, demonstrating that he could be other things. His mouth slid with continuing persuasion down her neck, lingering on the more sensory parts, which he found unerringly, pressing appeasingly against the frantically beating pulse at the base of her long white throat, as though all he sought to do was comfort her. His lips, lazily relaxed, softly damp, tormented her now with tenderness.

'Come.' Swiftly he picked her up, carrying her rapidly to her room and lowering her to the bed covered with satin cushions. He sat down beside her, still keeping her close. 'I will play the game your way, if this is what you want, *mignonne*. I'm in no great hurry. Should it take me one night or one week, your body knows it will be mine, even if your heart, as yet, refuses to acknowledge it.'

'Your fiancée?' Maxine groaned, her senses swimming while desperately aware that she must grasp at any weapon she could find. She must find some way of resisting his ruthless demands.

He merely laughed, as if he was no longer thinking of any other girl but herself. He was busy undoing the tiny buttons at the front of her brief blouse and, with her bones turning slowly to water, she could do nothing to prevent him. With the last of the buttons undone he pushed the filmy material off her shoulders and the pearly gleam of her breasts seemed to rivet him.

'You are beautiful, *chérie*.' His voice was deep and velvety, as his hand came out to mould the shape of her, his long, sensitive fingers caressing her gently at first, then with increasing urgency. His hands moved possessively over her body, arousing in her feelings she hadn't known about. Moaning, she clung to him and she heard his breathing quicken as he lowered himself over her.

As his heavy body crushed hers, his arms tightened and his head blotted out the light. His mouth hovered over her own, touching her lips lightly before taking full possession, and suddenly instead of fighting, as flames devoured her again, she found herself clinging to him, unable to think. Beyond hearing, she was also beyond caring, only wanting to know, with a devastating flare of desire, what lay over the brink.

'Kurt. . . .' she moaned, her arms lacing tightly around his strong neck, unaware that she had spoken his name for the first time.

The wild shouting outside went unheard at first. It was only when it drew nearer, increasing in volume, that Kurt released her. As he moved away from her, his dark face changed from passion to anger as he cursed impatiently, '*Mon dieu!* Someone will suffer for this!'

Dazed, her eyes dilated with emotion, Maxine watched him leave her. It was only then that she realised he was fully dressed, as indeed so was she, apart from the disarray of her blouse. Her cheeks burning, she struggled to the edge of the divan, a strange humiliation washing over her. It was quite obvious that he had not seriously intended making love to her, he had simply been amusing himself, apparently seeing how far she was prepared to let him go.

Overwhelmingly ashamed of herself because of the response she hadn't been able to hide, she covered her face with trembling hands. And the surge of longing she felt was so ridden with guilt as to be quickly suppressed and ignored.

After a few seconds, however, she lifted her head to stare at the walls of the tent, wishing she dared disobey Kurt's instructions about not leaving the room. She heard his voice, the deep tones carrying so much authority as to be unmistakable, then after another small spate of noise there was silence. Only one man's voice kept up a frenzied outcry, then even this faded in the distance, as though the culprit was being quickly removed. Once more there was only the haunting quiet, which was such a magical part of the desert night.

Crouched nervously among the cushions, Maxine waited for Kurt to return. A long time passed before she was convinced he couldn't be coming. It looked very much as if he had been called to settle the dispute, or whatever it was that had caused all the rumpus. He might be gone hours.

With mixed feelings of relief, Maxine tried to relax on her bed, while still incredibly stunned by the emotions Kurt had aroused inside her. How could it be that two people who disliked each other so much could react as they had done in each other's arms? Kurt d'Estier, she knew, must be experienced, but Maxine had never had a proper boy-friend. After the convent, where life had been very restricted, Mrs Martin had kept her busy, and there had been so much to learn. Apart from a few evenings at the theatre, of which Mrs Martin was passionately fond, and some business entertaining, Maxine had seldom been out. Mrs Martin had said recently that she must have some social life of her own, but so far nothing had been done about it. Certainly Maxine had had no idea it was possible to feel as she had done when Kurt had kissed her. When the one or two boys whom she had met at the rare party had done so, she hadn't felt a thing.

Still puzzling over this, she fell asleep, awakening at dawn to find Zara standing over her. Zara appeared to find it amusing that Maxine had slept fully clothed. Holding up a flimsy nightdress, she pointed to it, giggling.

Shaking back her tumbled hair from off her hot face, Maxine smiled uncertainly. Her thoughts suddenly racing backwards, she found herself wondering again what all the commotion had been about through the night. More anxious about this than the creased state of her clothes, she hurried to get out of bed, her heart thudding, almost painfully, as she tried to imagine what Kurt would have to say to her. What would the day bring?

Would he be more willing now to listen to the explanations he had previously not allowed her to express? To a man like Kurt d'Estier a few kisses might not mean a thing, but while she was bitterly aware of this it didn't prevent her completely from hoping.

Maxine hadn't long to wait. Almost before she had time to bath and change he was striding unannounced into her bedroom. Wearing a black shirt with a pair of tough-looking breeches, he looked more like a handsome brigand than ever. He looked well. Beneath his eyes were none of the dark shadows which encircled Maxine's, and irrationally she felt resentful. Somewhere, it was obvious, he had passed the night in peaceful tranquillity!

The resentment which showed on her face Kurt d'Estier put down to his entering so precipitately. His glance going swiftly over her, he bent his head mockingly, 'I apologise, *chérie*, but after all it is my tent. Perhaps you should put a notice on your door explaining the exact nature of what you are doing, then I will be better able to judge if it is safe for me to enter.'

'You might appreciate your jokes, but I don't,' she retorted truculently, not quite able to meet his eyes.

'Ah, my dear,' the mockery still lingered on his lips as he waved for Zara to be gone, 'I could have sworn you had a sense of humour. When I kissed you....'

Not yet feeling up to discussing this with him, she broke in, holding on desperately to a hint of aggression. 'Will you please tell me what's going on? It was scarcely considerate of you to leave me wondering all night. I couldn't decide whether the camp was being taken over by another tribe or not. You may laugh, *monsieur*, but we hear so much at home about the wars which go on all over this part of the world.'

'Was this all that kept you awake, Max?'

'What else should there be?'

Suddenly he had crossed the space between them, his arms reaching out to pull her close. As if this was not enough he put a hand under her chin, lifting it so he might see her face. 'I think, *mademoiselle*, this show of temper hides something other than fright? Or fright other than that caused by the ravings of a rabid nomad who wandered to our dark oasis in the night.'

'Oh, the poor man!' Swift compassion caused Maxine momentarily to forget her own problems. 'What did you do with him? I hope you were kind?'

'We have our own ways of dealing with such a crisis, and perhaps I was grateful to have something to keep me occupied. You can rest assured we did everything possible, but I'm afraid the man died.'

'I see.' Her eyes clouded, and through the turmoil within her at being held so close to Kurt's hard body, she felt curiously depressed. 'I suppose you have doctors?'

'Very good ones, when they are available,' he said dryly. 'But in this case, no doctor could have helped.'

When she made no reply, he moved his hand a little to caress her ear, 'Were you disappointed when I didn't return, *ma chère*?'

'No!' Suddenly aware of his hard muscles digging into her, she began struggling against him, hoping he couldn't feel how her heart was pounding. 'Will you stop using me,' she gasped, 'like some woman you've picked up off the streets!'

'You put ideas in my head,' he mocked, forcibly controlling her struggles. Holding her in an iron grip, he nuzzled her shoulder with his deeply clefted chin, until her pulse leapt uncontrollably. His eyes flickered over her with an insolence which sent the blood rushing to her cheeks, but when she began to protest, his mouth immediately clamped down on her parted lips.

Beneath the flaunting sensuality of his kiss her senses spun. Without remorse, he pushed aside her thin top, laying his hand over her full, curving breast. His thumb he spread over her racing heart as he raised his head. 'Is this because of me—or temper?' he asked.

'Let me go!' she spluttered, through shaking lips, with superhuman effort tearing herself away from him. 'You're just amusing yourself at my expense!'

'You're scarcely in the position to complain,' he taunted, but made no attempt to snatch her back to him again.

'You—you're despicable, *monsieur*! A fiend, a mad-man, a rogue! No wonder your....'

'You may well pause,' he said coldly. 'Repeat that again and you will find me all of those things you have mentioned.' Grasping her shoulders, he shook her. 'Don't try to pretend you're indifferent to me. I wouldn't believe you. And, as I've already pointed out, why shouldn't I enjoy what others have had before me?'

'No, *monsieur*....'

'Last night,' he recalled grimly, 'you had no difficulty in calling me Kurt. While I am not over-concerned with what you choose to call me, it makes a change from your continual *monsieurs*. I also found your warm-blooded response less irritating than your constant as-sertions that you've never known a man.'

'I didn't respond!' Maxine glared at him defiantly, attempting to cover a trembling weakness with anger. 'You were so carried away by your own confidence, *monsieur*, that you didn't realise I was only trying to escape you.'

Making no effort to hide a sneer, he exclaimed, 'If I had more time this morning I would quickly prove to you the folly of your words, Miss Martin. You are no shrinking spinster, *chérie*, but perhaps no man has ever taken the trouble to convince you. This morning I am not able to change my plans, but I look forward to seeing you later. Before the evening is out I promise you will be calling me something very different from *monsieur*, or any of the other names you use so freely.'

'I don't understand you,' she whispered, backing away from him, flinching from his cold, merciless eyes.

'It isn't necessary,' he answered curtly, all former traces of good humour gone. He looked grim and hard. Caustically he regarded her shrinking figure as he prepared to leave. On his lips was an open sneer. 'Just be ready to welcome me back, that's all.'

For the whole day Maxine alternated between anger and despair, not knowing how seriously to take his arrogant threats. If he loved his fiancée, surely he couldn't be thinking of involving himself with another girl? Maxine was startled to find herself regarding his fiancée almost enviously. She was further surprised by a distinct feeling of jealousy. What must it be like to be loved by a man like Kurt d'Estier? Shivering, she put such thoughts from her. When he found his fiancée he wouldn't be able to get rid of Maxine quickly enough, and she would probably never see him again.

Although Kurt had gone she found she wasn't confined to the tent. Relieved about this, if nothing else, Maxine spent the morning wandering around the encampment. Most of the men appeared to have gone with Kurt, but the women remained. Many of these were veiled, as they went quietly about their daily work. They were too busy to take much notice of the young English girl who wandered in their midst, but above their black veils their eyes were kind, if a little curious.

The woman who had served their dinner the previous night was never far from her side. Whether or not this was on Kurt's instructions, Maxine failed to find out. Certainly she was pleasant enough, and very obliging when the heat caused Maxine to ask frequently for a drink of water. But when it came to information the woman either didn't know or had been given orders not to tell. Maxine suspected the latter, as when she asked how far it was to the nearest town she received no answer. Which, as Kurt had mentioned how these people knew the desert like the palms of their hands, didn't seem to make sense. The woman merely looked away and shook her head.

There wasn't a great deal to see, nothing to take Maxine's mind off the unfortunate position she was in. Often she had longed to travel but could find little pleasure in seeing the world as she was doing now— with the threat of disaster hanging constantly over her. She now wished fervently she had followed her first instincts and refused to come to Casablanca. If she had just been an ordinary tourist she might have found the desert interesting, even absorbing. But as the prisoner of a man wholly motivated by a desire for revenge, she found it difficult to relax, for even a few minutes.

When, with her mind exploring every possible way of escape, she enquired discreetly if they could communicate with Marrakesh from the camp, the woman with her again said no.

'Is it not possible to get in touch with anyone?' Maxine asked, trying to conceal her exasperation.

'You ask the Sidi when he returns,' was all the woman would say.

Maxine was sure Kurt must have some means of keeping in touch with his business, but it was obvious she wasn't going to learn of it this way. Pretending an interest she didn't really feel, she explored the oasis again, but could find nothing that might remotely help her. Apart from a few pathetic goats and lambs, kept for a purpose she preferred not to think about, there was only the scattered black tents, full of chattering women and children. Short of running over the desert, which she knew would be committing suicide, she had no means of escaping from her prison.

It was late when Kurt returned that evening; she grew almost weary of waiting for him. She had bathed and changed, not from any desire to please him, but because even with the greatest care clothing quickly became sticky here with dust and perspiration. This evening she wore a pair of soft blue trousers with a matching top, the brief bodice being sewn with tiny silver sequins and pearls. Zara had found a matching band to confine her hair, which brought a welcome coolness to the nape of her neck. The hours in the sun had given to Maxine's skin a faint bloom of pink which was very becoming, and distracted from the soft violet shadows which apprehension had painted under her grey eyes.

When at last Kurt arrived he didn't surprise her as she heard his horses approaching the tent. The thud of hooves was not to be mistaken. This, along with the jingle of bridles and heavy voices of men, suggested they had ridden far and hard, and she hoped that Kurt would be too weary to taunt her unduly that night. She was in the main room when he strode in. Having heard his terse orders she wasn't surprised to see him followed immediately by a servant carrying water.

'Good evening, Miss Martin,' his eyes went swiftly over her, her slender beauty making him pause in approval, if it was only expressed by the extra glint in his eye. 'I see you are waiting for your dinner. Give me ten minutes to clean up.'

With a slight smile for her increasing colour, he disappeared behind one of the thin partitions which divided the rooms. As Maxine tried to compose herself against a rush of inexplicable emotion, her ears were filled with the sound of splashing water, the vigorous swish of towels, all the embarrassingly unfamiliar sounds of a man removing the outward signs of a hard day's work. True to his word, he was little more than the few minutes he had allocated himself, and when he joined her he hadn't the appearance of someone despondent over losing their fiancée.

'Did you find her, *monsieur?*' She was so certain this was what he had been trying to do that she kept her sentence brief. It was a rather silly question, she realised, as if he had found his fiancée she would have been with him. Without wondering why, Maxine felt strangely relieved that she wasn't yet to meet her.

'Does it look like it?' he jeered, confirming her suspicions that he would have brought the girl with him.

'I only wondered,' Maxine swallowed a peculiar lump in her throat. Again he was wearing white silky trousers, but tonight his tunic was open almost down to his waist. She was aghast to find she couldn't look at him with any equanimity.

'No.' This time his voice was decisive as he sat down beside her. As if they had some mysterious means of judging the exact moment, servants appeared with their food. 'Allah be praised,' he smiled grimly. 'I haven't broken my fast since this morning, *chérie*, and I am hungry, very hungry!'

Enigmatically his glance rested on Maxine's full, curved lips, and she hoped, with an uncontrollable flash of panic, that he wasn't thinking of her as well.

After serving the food the servants quietly withdrew, leaving behind an uncomfortable silence. Thinking of the little lambs outside, Maxine found herself staring at the food without appetite.

'Aren't you going to eat anything?' Kurt asked, gazing at her keenly. 'Meat here is something of a luxury, you know. You will offend these people greatly if you refuse what they have taken so much trouble to prepare.'

Lowering her head, she tried to explain. 'It's just that this morning I saw the small lambs penned up, *monsieur*.'

'And you can't forget them,' he added astutely, as she paused. He sighed tightly. 'This is a little different from England, you are finding? There, there might well be no connection between the pretty lambs gambolling in the green fields and the carcasses hanging in your butchers' shops. You might find life in the desert primitive, *chérie*, but at least it is down-to-earth. What use would a butcher's shop be to these people, who might easily be hundreds of miles away from the nearest one. And how could meat be prevented from going bad, in temperatures of often over a hundred and thirty degrees, unless it was kept alive until needed?'

'I didn't mean to criticise,' Maxine replied in a very small voice.

Very slightly he relented. 'Ignorance is perhaps responsible for most of the criticism levelled by strangers in this land. In any land, I suppose, come to that. But, actually, *ma petite*, to the average nomad meat is a luxury he can seldom afford. Mostly he lives on dates and cereals of rice and maize—a diet which few Europeans would tolerate.'

'But there are rich Moroccans—Arabs in the Middle East, who are better off?' she said uncertainly.

'Plenty,' he agreed. 'But the Middle East is also swarming with the poor and lowly. Governments try all the time to raise the general standard of living, but mostly the land is too poor to support a healthy economy.'

'I have heard of irrigation schemes in the desert?'

Kurt's sigh reached her wryly. 'We have many of these, but it means a constant fight against the supremacy of nature. Also with the nature of the people. Most of the desert tribes are wanderers at heart; they don't wish to settle in any one spot.'

Maxine frowned. 'If they enjoy their present way of life, why change it?'

His eyes met hers sardonically. 'I believe it was you who advocated the change, if only indirectly, not me. You were almost weeping over your dinner, *mademoiselle*. I feel your heart needs to be harder.'

'Yes,' she found herself smiling back, half ruefully. 'But, apart from the lambs, there's a lot here in the desert which makes me curious. When I was out, this morning, *monsieur*, I watched the people carefully. They may be poor and underprivileged, but they are always smiling. Their eyes are kind and they seem content with their lot, and I don't believe it's because they are ignorant.'

'It seems you have observed closely.'

Filled with a warm enthusiasm, Maxine didn't notice his slight sarcasm. 'I think they have too many children, but their mothers seem to have plenty of love and patience. They even seemed to have some to spare for me, and I'm a stranger.'

'You are my woman,' he corrected her sardonically, his dark eyes mocking. 'That alone would ensure you a welcome. Our children they will expect to see later.'

Her face went hot, her animosity back, the sympathy between them forgotten. In a way she was glad of her anger, as it quickly put a stop to the odd warmth she had began to feel towards him. Sharply she said, 'I suppose, if they think I'm your property, they wouldn't dare do anything else but welcome me.'

'I wouldn't attach too much importance to it, if I were you,' he drawled carelessly. 'A few more days and we move on. They will forget you as easily as they do the wind, which blows one minute and is gone the next.'

Hopefully, she asked, 'So you don't intend staying?'

'Only as long as it takes.'

Puzzled, Maxine stared at him over the rim of her coffee cup. Her hands tightened around it, then she put it down carefully. 'As long as it takes to find Colin and your fiancée, you mean?'

'No,' he explained coldly, holding her eyes. 'As long as it takes to teach you a lesson, Miss Martin.'

'What kind of a lesson, *monsieur*?' The tremor in her voice betrayed her fear, in spite of the direct frankness of her query.

For a few moments he went on looking at her, and to her relief his face seemed to soften. 'Oh, nothing too drastic,' he said suavely, 'nothing you won't enjoy. I intend keeping you here just long enough to give your family a fright. As I have said, none of you can expect to escape some form of reprisal.'

This didn't sound too bad. Maxine breathed a sigh

which contained some relief. His bark might be worse than his bite, as with many people, his outrageous threats only meant to scare. With another relieved sigh which was audible, she nodded, not attempting to debate the fairness of his last statement. No longer did she feel it was greatly imperative to try and impress on him her true identity. Instead she used her newly formed confidence to ask about something which had been worrying her increasingly all day.

'What made Colin go off with your fiancée, *mon-sieur*?'

Immediately she regretted her apparent inability to leave Kurt's affairs alone. His face went cold, but to her surprise he didn't altogether refuse to answer. Only for a moment did he hesitate, his eyes narrowed, as if he was wondering how much he should tell her. 'I might have been able to forgive him, *mademoiselle*, if I had been convinced that he loved her. This I am sure he did not. For years he has been striving in vain to prove his superiority over me and failed. Perhaps he saw this as his last opportunity? He played on the feelings of a bored woman, until she was apparently willing to agree to anything.'

Maxine frowned. 'How could she be bored, when she was engaged to you, *monsieur*?' she exclaimed without thinking.

He smiled savagely, his eyes on her perplexed face. 'You appear to find this difficult to believe. But then,' he mused cynically, 'you were never bored with me, during our short acquaintance. It was a long time ago, but I haven't forgotten how much you wanted me. Now I intend finding out if you still do. Come here, *mignonne*.'

CHAPTER FIVE

I⟶ was a command which Maxine wasn't prepared to obey, and when Kurt saw how she intended to defy him he leant across the low sofa on which they sat and pulled her to him. 'I think I know sufficient about women to make a satisfactory lover,' he assured her coolly.

'No, Kurt, please! For heaven's sake!' she cried, trying to find the strength to speak sensibly, to preserve her fast fading sanity. Making a great effort to ignore the feel of his hands on her bare arms, she lifted her shining head to look at him. 'Wouldn't it be better if I left you? You could have the rest of the night to yourself. We only fight, and you can't find that very relaxing.'

'I have no wish to spend the rest of the night alone, *ma chérie*,' he mocked her.

As his eyes glittered his grip tightened, and panic overwhelmed the composure she had been attempting to hang on on. Quickly she jumped to her feet, jerking away from him, taking him by surprise. But she didn't manage more than two or three steps before he caught her, his face darkening with an all too familiar anger.

Savagely his arms claimed her, lifting her half off her feet, disregarding the dry sob in her throat as he crushed her to him. Then he bent his tall head and took her defenceless mouth, in a kiss of such ruthlessness that she knew he was still consumed by an overwhelming desire for revenge.

Desperately, as on the previous evening, she tried to fight him, but was hampered as much by her own spinning senses as his iron hold on her slender body. In spite of this she managed to hit out at him with small, clenched fists, until he grabbed her flailing arms.

When she resorted to kicking him, he simply picked her up, confining her writhing limbs hard against him. 'Stop it!' his fingers bit into her menacingly, as he released her numbed lips. 'I'm getting more than tired of this pose of yours, this pretence of innocence.'

Shooting him a furious glance—all she dared allow herself with his hard face thrust so near—she gasped, 'You're stronger than I am, but you can't stop me from speaking my mind. You might not believe it, as you've such a high opinion of yourself, but I certainly don't want you for a—a lover!'

'So you're aiming higher now?' The edge of his mouth gave a contemptuous quirk. 'A husband, perhaps? You wouldn't expect me to marry you, *mignonne*?'

'I don't expect anything of the sort,' her voice was tense with the peculiar agony inside her, 'I just want to be left alone!'

He spoke with sudden harshness. 'Before trying to discipline your mind, girl, you should have started on your enticing body. It is so used to a lover that it responds to mine exactly.'

'You're mad!' she shouted, her attitude defiantly defensive, her pulse racing, with what she chose to believe was fright.

'Then we both are,' he taunted, dragging her instantly closer again, crushing his mouth against her lips and welding them together with a hard, savage passion, a fervour all the more frightening because of the leaping response she failed to control.

She felt the fire and urgency of his need and the world faded. As his hands moulded her to him, his hard body seemed to sear hers all the way down, as if, in the heat of his desire, he wanted to fuse her to him. She couldn't move, she soon lost the will to. Her eyes closed and she went limp, as his mouth, moist and urgent, drove her half crazy. His lips discovered the shape of hers before pressing them open. There was a faint hint of coffee on his breath as his lips searched hungrily, and with a groan Maxine's arms went up to cling to his broad shoulders.

'Maxine!' he muttered thickly, easing his mouth on a deeply drawn breath. '*Mon dieu*, you're beautiful! I don't seem to remember! I must have been a fool, but in the name of Allah stop playing with me.'

Maxine felt, if she didn't wholly understand, the muscles of his hard, vigorous body contracting. And deep within her came identical tremors, as she knew for the first time in her life what it was to want a man. It became an ache, too much to bear, bringing a longing she found difficult to ignore. His hands, as though intent on bringing her to an irrevocable decision, slipped into her brief top. He touched her breasts, his mouth lowering to follow his initial explorations, softly, relentlessly caressing.

She felt his nostrils tense at the scent of her warm skin, and was suddenly unable to resist him. Turning her head, she was kissing him in return, pressing feverish lips to the side of his neck, the hard smoothness of his cheek, the pulse which throbbed at his temple. Arching, unconsciously seductive to the impatient demands of his body, she almost begged aloud to have his mouth on hers again. As the world turned upside down, the fire in her blood melted her last bit of resistance.

'Tonight,' Kurt said softly, surveying her flushed face, 'there will be no more interruptions. You will belong to me, every part of you.'

Like a blow falling, she was suddenly shocked. 'No. . . .' If he hadn't said anything she doubted if she would have been able to fight him, but the total commitment he spoke of seemed to jar the innocence within her. It made her ashamed, even while her senses clamoured to surrender. 'No, Kurt. Not like this,' she pleaded weakly.

Arrogantly, his eyes boring into her, he rejoined

harshly, 'I won't send you back to England until you are —what would you call it—completely compromised, *chérie*. That will be a scandal which perhaps your mother will not enjoy.'

The full horror of what he was saying didn't penetrate immediately, then panic stricken she wrenched away from him. Yet for a moment she couldn't think he could mean what she thought he did. 'I don't believe you realise what you're saying!' she cried, her face white.

'You think not?' he said cuttingly, his eyes raking her without pity.

'You're insane!' she whispered, feeling suddenly faint.

Coolly he stood watching her, his dark eyes frosting over. 'No woman would ever drive me insane, *petite*, but I believe I could make you that way.'

'I refuse to let you touch me!' Wildly she backed from him, wholly stunned by what she had learnt of his ruthless intentions. At the same time she felt oddly tormented.

He merely smiled at her hysterical words as he followed her retreat, the strength of his hard body reflected in the firm set of his mouth. Within inches of her he stopped. 'Don't worry, my dear, I have no intention of forcing myself on you—not yet. Suddenly I feel bored with all this fighting. You weren't fighting that night I caught you in Moulay ben Hassoun's arms, which proves, does it not, that you can be bought if not persuaded? But I will do neither, *chérie*. I will simply wait until you come begging. Which won't be much longer, if your delightful little display of passion a few minutes ago is anything to go by.'

Her face chalky, her hands shaking, Maxine stared at him. Putting out a scornful hand, he caught her chin. 'What a wonderful actress you are, Maxine! You manage, at thirty, to look sixteen, and now you're trying to turn yourself into a convincing virgin. I'll admit I occasionally find it hard to believe you share the same duplicity as your brother, but facts don't lie.'

Maxine tried to speak but couldn't. She felt like cry-ing, but no tears came. She wanted to hit out at him for the cruel things he said, while at the same time she knew an urge to cling, to tell him she could understand his contempt and forgive it, as she wasn't the girl he thought she was.

But even as such thoughts spun through her head, the condemnation in his eyes kept her silent. She swallowed convulsively as a single tear ran down her pale cheeks, and unsteadily she raised a slender hand to brush it away. In his arms she had been about to whisper some-thing very different from the cynical words which had just fallen from his lips. Words which might have be-trayed her so completely that he wouldn't have hesitated in taking his own way. She could feel grateful now that his anger had at least prevented this happening.

'Go to your bed, Miss Martin.' A little of the grimness left his face as he watched her, as his voice cut through her thoughts sardonically. 'Don't let the past worry you unduly. As I said last night, I have plenty of patience. It's not as though you were going anywhere, *ma chère.*'

Maxine might have been thankful that forthcoming events proved him wrong, if the news which was re-sponsible for her leaving the oasis hadn't been so devasta-tingly tragic!

She went to bed, as he advised, but couldn't sleep. Through the darkness she was haunted by the terrible suspicion that even if Kurt never came near her again she wasn't going to escape from Morocco unscathed. She wasn't sure what she felt for Kurt d'Estier. He was good-looking enough to turn any woman's head, and this, combined with a cool, arrogant confidence, gave him an aura which few would be able to resist. But to imagine she loved him must be crazy! What she was suffering from could be nothing more than a schoolgirl crush, brought on by the romantic if slightly unreal atmosphere of the desert. She might have reason to be grateful that the discovery of Kurt's true motives for keeping her here had shocked any such fancies right out of her mind.

The next morning, wishing only to leave her tumbled bed, she slipped out into the dawn. She wasn't sure of the hour but suspected it had been daylight for some time, although there was still some freshness in the air. Away from the tent she breathed deeply, pulling her cloak lightly around her as she walked a little distance from the oasis. Either Kurt wasn't up or he was busy elsewhere, for she could see nothing of him, and she was grateful to have even a few minutes to herself.

The helicopter, when it came, appeared to whirl straight at her over the top of a huge sand dune. If she had been listening, Maxine supposed she might have heard it, but it took her completely by surprise. To her astonishment, after flying over her head, it landed on a level patch of ground about a hundred yards away. Instinctively, without pausing to think, she ran towards it. It could be a means of escape which might never come again.

Unfortunately Kurt was there before her, striding over the sands, his face like thunder. Typical! she thought, quick hatred in her heart. Why was it she could never get the better of him?

'Go back to camp at once!' he commanded grimly, as she struggled up to him.

Maxine stood where she was, although her heart beat over rapidly. 'You'll have to carry me first!' she retorted, flinging back her hair and staring at him defiantly.

'In a moment I will,' he returned her cool regard succinctly. 'You're going to be sorry, chérie, very sorry indeed for defying me, after I've dealt with this fool in the helicopter.'

The man whom he spoke of so disparagingly was busy climbing from his machine. He must have overheard.

Maxine saw he was a pleasant-looking man, maybe a year or so older than Kurt d'Estier. If he had hoped for a welcome he didn't find it in Kurt's grim face, but this didn't appear to deter him.

'Good morning, Kurt,' he said, on reaching the ground, his eyes flickering over Maxine curiously.

Kurt didn't effect an introduction, nor did he return the greetings. 'What the hell do you think you're doing?' he asked curtly. 'I told you not to come here.'

'I'm sorry,' the man took out a large handkerchief to rub the sweat from his brow. 'I know you did, Kurt, I'm not a fool, but I have news which I felt I must bring to you personally.'

'I see.' A sudden wariness came over Kurt's features as he frowned, as though he had guessed what kind of news his friend was bringing.

The man went on, after another quick glance at Maxine, 'I think you might prefer to be alone.'

Abruptly Kurt turned to Maxine. 'You will go back to camp.' He made no attempt to introduce her, even now.

Hastily Maxine tried to collect her wits. '*Monsieur*,' she spoke quickly to the man, but Kurt immediately forestalled her.

Obviously anticipating such a contingency, he lifted his hand to a group of Berbers standing behind them. He said something in their own language and she found herself surrounded.

Their intention was so clear that she went pale. 'It's quite all right,' she gasped sharply at Kurt's impassive face, 'you don't have to use force. I'm quite capable of walking.' Her cheeks burning with humiliation, she turned away, to be escorted like a defecting prisoner back to the tent. She couldn't imagine what the stranger must be thinking, but she hoped desperately that he might guess something of her predicament and try to help.

She didn't see anything more of Kurt until later that

day. The helicopter hadn't stayed long. After about half an hour she heard it leaving, taking with it every hope she had been harbouring of escape. Tense with nervous frustration, she moved restlessly about the tent. She had a hollow feeling that the stranger had brought news of Colin Martin and Kurt's fiancée, and was soon over-wrought with anxiety. If something dreadful had happened, and Mrs Martin was alone when she heard of it, what on earth would she do? And, if they had been found safe and well, what would Kurt do? He hadn't been near her since the helicopter left, so perhaps he was already preparing to go and meet them.

A frown creased Maxine's brow as she considered what a terrible ordeal this would be for him, having to drag the woman he loved from the arms of another man or, worse still, to be rejected by her again! For the first time since she had known him, Maxine's heart ached for him. Even if his fiancée had returned and Kurt found he could forgive her, would he ever be able to forget the unhappiness she had caused him? She shivered, a sob in her throat, wishing it was in her power to spare Kurt this possible heartache. Not once did she stop to consider the ruthless way he had treated her.

It was after noon when at last he came striding into the tent. All morning she had been imprisoned in it by two guards, standing outside the door, but she had made no attempt to go out, knowing it to be hopeless. Even she knew that the burning stretches of desert sand would prove a worse deterrent than a hundred men, but she had wondered what was going on around the oasis that Kurt didn't want her to know about. Or had he only wanted to keep her out of the way until he had recovered from whatever he had learnt from the stranger?

When he did come he might have looked a little grimmer, but otherwise was much the same as usual. It wasn't until she saw his eyes, and he spoke, that her heart began thudding with fear.

He began without preamble, his voice expressionless, 'This morning I have received news which has meant making arrangements to leave immediately.'

'Immediately?' Why did the word suddenly fill her with dread? 'Where are we going?'

'Back to the ksar. Where you were before we came here,' his icy glance went over her. 'You'd better bring your burnous as the helicopter will be coming for us at any minute.'

'Kurt?' Going up to him, she laid an urgent hand on his arm, unable to contain her curiosity any longer, 'What did that man want? Who is he?'

'Someone who works for me.' He didn't answer her query directly but continued to stare at her coldly. 'A man I would trust with my life.'

'You didn't seem very pleased to see him.' She was puzzled, recalling the tone of Kurt's welcome.

Kurt paused, on his way to his room, his face harshly intolerant. 'Haven't I just said he works for me? He had orders not to come here.'

'Didn't the news which he brought justify the breaking of these orders?' Maxine stammered.

'Yes.'

He said no more, and she felt a terrible uneasiness as she did as he instructed. Collecting her burnous, she followed him from the tent. On leaving she was consumed by a strange nostalgia which surprised her. She had thought she hated this place, would be delighted to see the last of it, yet something had happened to her here. While it wasn't altogether clear what it was, she knew she would never again be quite so young and naïve as the girl who had first come to this oasis.

Kurt strode ahead, the set of his broad shoulders so unyielding she was filled with alarm. Something was very wrong. It was as if he had sustained a shock, which might have felled another man.

'Monsieur?' She hurried to keep up with his long

stride. 'I don't wish to sound impertinent, but was the news about Colin, or perhaps your business?'

'Be quiet, can't you!' he snarled, without pity for her shortening breath, or her almost tearful anxiety. 'I'll satisfy your curiosity fully when we get back to the ksar, but not before. I promise all will soon be explained.'

When Maxine considered their previous journey, to the oasis, the considerable discomfort they had endured, she was surprised that Kurt hadn't used the helicopter before. But when she gathered enough courage to ask him about it, he merely shrugged. 'When I travel in the desert I use this kind of transport as little as possible.'

'Why not?' With such a frightening uncertainty rampaging inside her, Maxine was sure that if she didn't stick to ordinary topics she might go crazy, and to sit too long with her own thoughts might produce the same result.

'The questions you ask! *Mon dieu*, is there no end to them?' His voice was terse with impatience, yet a quick glance at Maxine's taut face seemed to convince him that her control was only held by a thread and he answered her. 'I prefer keeping to the ways these people are familiar with. I cannot say more than this. Did you find your trip out so uncomfortable?'

'No.' She was startled to find this was almost the truth. In other circumstances she would have enjoyed it. There had been something exciting and strangely satisfying about sleeping under the stars. She could still feel the night wind caressing her cheeks and see the huge moon overhead. It hadn't been all pleasure, but she was young enough to endure, even enjoy a few hardships. No, if it hadn't been for what had lain behind such a journey, she would never have grumbled about it. 'I didn't find it too uncomfortable,' she admitted stiffly. Then, with a rush of young candour, 'I might even have thought it fun, if I hadn't been a prisoner.'

This didn't appear to bother Kurt d'Estier one bit. He

lapsed into silence which, this time, Maxine forced herself to put up with. He was obviously preoccupied, and she wondered if he would be prepared to enlighten her when they arrived at the ksar. Somehow she could feel it in her bones that the news he had received wasn't good!

It was late afternoon when they reached their destination. Immediately Kurt removed her from the machine, before she had a chance to speak to the pilot. The pilot wasn't the same man who had been at the oasis that morning, although the helicopter was of a similar design. Maxine could only assume that when the first man had returned to wherever he had come from, he had, on Kurt's orders, sent this other pilot back in his stead.

As she walked resignedly towards the ksar she heard Kurt speaking in rapid French to the man before he came after her. The helicopter, she noticed, didn't take off again, and hope flared suddenly in her heart. Could it be that he was waiting to take them back to Casablanca? Kurt was devious, he also hated her. He wouldn't willingly provide the comfort such information would give to the girl whose family he considered had wronged him!

Inside the huge, castle-like structure all was quiet. In the high, wide hallway, the faithful Izaak came bowing to meet them and was instantly dismissed. Kurt waved an impatient hand after asking one abrupt question and receiving a swift answer. Then he drew Maxine into a small nearby room.

'We have to talk, Maxine, and quickly. We don't have much time to spare if the helicopter is to leave before dark.'

While this ought to have given strength to her hopes of leaving, somehow it didn't. She waited, not this time having anything to say, but a kind of unconscious dread darkened her grey eyes as Izaak brought in a tray of coffee. Dully she wondered why Kurt had bothered with it if he was in such a hurry.

Again Izaak was abruptly dismissed and, as Kurt poured the coffee, she noticed how his face remained grim. Suddenly she wished he would get on with whatever it was he had to tell her. Her nerves were strung tightly and she felt a sharp panic rising, which she might not be able to control much longer.

All desire for coffee fading, she shook her head slowly when he offered her a cup. 'You'd better take it, my dear,' he advised coldly. 'You might need it.'

'Please, Kurt,' she entreated, as though begging him to stop tormenting her thus, but he didn't say anything more until she had taken the small cup and drained the contents. She noticed he didn't have any himself, but found it difficult to believe he had only been thinking of her.

'Now,' he said curtly, as she stared up at him mutely, after replacing the cup in its small, ornamental saucer, 'I will tell you what you are so anxious to know. Noel Franck, the man who came to the oasis this morning, did bring news. Bad news. Word about my fiancée and your brother.'

Maxine went cold, but could only think of poor Mrs Martin. 'Oh, no!' she gasped.

'They have both been killed.' He made no attempt to soften the blow.

'But how?' Maxine moved her stiff lips with difficulty.

He might have been discussing something which had nothing to do with him, his voice was so steely impassive. 'They were on their way to Mexico, apparently, when the plane crashed.'

Stunned with shock, Maxine could scarcely bring herself to believe it. Her face went white, and she was vaguely glad she had had the coffee. Colin had been selfish, in many ways irresponsible, but surely he hadn't deserved this! Then she remembered that Kurt had lost his fiancée. 'I'm sorry, *monsieur*,' she whispered hoarsely, wishing fervently that she could help him. Her eyes widened with quick compassion. 'You must have loved her very much. It's a terrible thing to have happened. You must be heartbroken. . . .'

He frowned in distaste, making it clear he didn't intend discussing his feelings with anyone. 'I don't think we'll waste time on the usual condolences, Miss Martin. They were both old enough to know exactly what they were doing.'

'Yes. All the same. . . .' Before his harsh stare, Maxine faltered into silence, making an obvious attempt to restrain her pity. 'I must go straight back to London. There must be a lot I can do to help.' Mrs Martin would be distraught. While she might have spoiled Colin, she had loved him very much. Maxine felt overwhelmed with sadness, for the good nuns had taught her that it was right to care about other people, and she was naturally kindhearted. She said quickly, 'It's still a dreadful thing to have happened, *monsieur*, and I must make arrangements to go home. Anyway, you won't want me here.'

She hoped he didn't detect the odd bleakness in her voice. For a moment, as he looked at her, she fancied he did, and she lowered her eyes so he shouldn't read anything more in them. To leave him, not to see him again, wasn't bringing any of the relief she expected, and she felt confused. Yet what could she do? He wouldn't so much as accept her sympathy. From her he didn't appear to want anything, not even that. Her heart flooded with pity at the sight of his grim face. She couldn't think of anything else. To leave him like this might be impossible. Surely he was in need of somebody?

Kurt continued to gaze at her contemptuously as she tried to find words to express something of what she was feeling, but when eventually he spoke she was so horrified that all her compassion fled. 'You won't be going anywhere, Maxine, not yet. You certainly won't be returning to England until you have my ring on your finger.'

'Your ring, *monsieur*?' As he towered over her, so tall and dark in his flowing white burnous, she felt herself go cold.

'Yes, my ring,' he repeated, as if he were speaking to someone slow of understanding. 'We are to be married, Maxine, this afternoon. Within the hour, as a matter of fact. The good priest is waiting.'

'Married!' A terrible sickness rose inside her, as she examined his face closely to see that he was merely teasing her. 'Are you crazy, *monsieur*? Is this some poor kind of joke?'

'No joke, Miss Martin.' He appeared to find some malignant amusement in anticipating the trembling accusation which came to her lips. 'No, I don't love you. In normal circumstances I would never marry a girl with your reputation, but I don't intend letting such a chance slip through my fingers.'

'What chance, *monsieur*?' Maxine continued to stare at him, trying desperately to hang on to her shaking composure, which she felt was in danger of going completely. He couldn't be serious! He must just be taking a last opportunity to torment her.

He laughed softly, his insolent glance taking pleasure in her shocked face as he answered her taut query. 'The chance to make the Martin family suffer for the wrong they have done me, perhaps. My fiancée, Maxine, was a wealthy woman, having inherited a great deal of money. Now I see a way to compensate myself for what your brother has done to me. You will, I believe, now inherit everything your mother has to leave, which must be considerable.'

'You can't be serious!' She was too stunned to take in exactly what this meant but was convinced more than ever that the shock he had sustained regarding his fiancée must have at least temporarily deranged him.

'Absolutely!' His decisiveness was such it could not be mistaken. 'Your family have used me despicably, Maxine, especially when, without me, they could never have survived. When I took you to the desert it was to make you suffer a little for your brother's sins. I see now how fate has played into my hands. It will amuse me, *chérie*, to see your mother's face when I present you as my wife. Of course she may decide to sell out and give her money to charity, but I could break her before she could take such a step.'

'Why not buy her out right away?' Maxine cried. 'Without Colin I don't think she will have the heart to go on.'

His eyebrows rose tauntingly. 'Why should I go to the expense of buying her out, when by marrying you I will get it all for nothing? Don't worry, *chérie*,' he sneered, cruelly, 'I think you will find your mother has enough confidence in my business ability to more than welcome me as her son-in-law.'

Suddenly Maxine started, wondering why she was getting in such a state. 'You must know, Kurt, I'm not Mrs Martin's daughter. I've been trying to convince you of this since I came here, but you refuse to listen.'

His dark eyes glittering with anger, he cut in, 'Stop wasting both my time and your own, girl. I won't warn you again.'

'But, Kurt, I only have the same name! I told you. . . .'

The anger in his eyes leapt, startling her to a frightened silence. 'You will not utter another word!'

Quaking with fear, she stared like a hypnotised rabbit, having little doubt that he would resort to violence, if need be, to get his own way. Before his contempt, a perverse devil of insanity ran through her shaking body. Why should she try any further to convince him of anything? Why not allow him the unpleasant shock of discovering the truth for himself, as he undoubtedly would? He was so sure of himself that not even the losing of his fiancée to another man had shaken his confidence. Wasn't it time something did? Perhaps he had a lesson to learn as well as other people?

Yet marriage to him was out of the question. Maxine knew; no matter how much she toyed with the desire for revenge, she couldn't do it. His kisses were one thing. The peculiar magnetism which existed between Kurt and herself made these resemble a particularly potent wine which, once tasted, made one crave for more. But marriage involved much more than a few kisses, and with the distrust they shared Maxine couldn't feel it would do either of them any good. And, if she had to struggle constantly with panic now, what would she be reduced to in the future, married to a man who hated her?

Disobeying his instructions not to utter another word, she tried to find another way of deterring him. 'When Mrs Martin discovers how you practically abducted me she'll go to the police.'

He smiled detestably. 'I shall tell her you jumped at the chance of marrying me.'

Mrs Martin would believe that. She was all too ready to believe people would do anything for money. It was because she was so fond of it herself. Dully Maxine heard Kurt adding:

'I think she knew you would have married me years ago, if I'd asked you, and since you came here no one has heard you screaming for help.'

Mortified, she whispered, 'Simply because I would have been wasting my breath!'

'You aren't totally unresponsive in my arms,' his voice might have softened slightly, 'In fact, chérie, I think once we are married, your feelings may surprise you. Over the years you have changed.'

'No!' Wild panic kept attacking her in waves, for she

was very young and frightened. He didn't realise how frightened, as he imagined her ten years older than she actually was.

'Come,' Kurt commanded, seemingly at the end of his patience, his glance smouldering, 'the priest awaits us, as does the pilot to take him back to his home.'

'Please!' Maxine made one final attempt to persuade him of his folly. She was about to insist that he checked up on her, when the floor suddenly began heaving under her feet, the walls twisting before her very eyes, and she found herself caught in Kurt's arms as she fainted.

In vain she tried to push him away, to bring the room back into focus, but it still whirled about her. 'Kurt,' she whispered, a sob in her voice, 'I can't seem to see properly.'

'It doesn't matter,' his voice came from a distance, although he held her closely, 'perhaps it is better like this. Just do exactly as I tell you.'

Laying her carefully on a couch, he left her, returning a few minutes later with Izaak, who carried something in a glass. Kneeling on one knee beside her, Kurt raised her head. 'Drink this,' he said, 'and you'll soon feel better.'

Not able to do anything but what she was told, Maxine found herself obeying feebly, but contrary to his assurance the drink seemed to make her feel worse instead of better. While she didn't lose consciousness again, the ability to focus properly didn't return. She grew alarmed. 'Kurt,' she entreated, clinging to his hands, 'please don't leave me!'

Staring down at her pale face, he studied her intently. Then, as she began to relax, he gently released his hands and put his arms around her, not remonstrating even when she hung on to him, like someone drowning.

When he told her they were to be married immediately, she made no further protest. 'Just repeat what the priest tells you,' he said slowly. 'You will also know when to say yes. I assure you, *ma chérie*, everything is going to be all right.'

Later, much later, when the world stopped spinning, Maxine discovered she was a married woman. She had tried appealing to the priest, but whatever Kurt had put in her drink had deprived her of the ability to speak her mind. She puzzled as to why he hadn't given her something straight away, but suspected he had hoped she would agree to marrying him without having to be over-persuaded. Angry frustration made her tremble as she realised she had made all the right responses, and the priest had appeared to believe she was merely suffering from a touch of heat-stroke.

The man had gone to great lengths to assure her he was properly ordained. He even gave the name of the city church where he could be contacted at any time. Maxine had nodded hazily, not too bemused to understand what he was saying, but not yet recovered sufficiently to fully comprehend the enormity of what was happening.

It wasn't until after the priest had gone and Kurt asked mockingly how she felt about being his wife that she fully realised what had taken place.

'You've tricked me!' she cried, her grey eyes stormy with anger. 'You're nothing but a low-down....'

'Don't say it,' he warned, grabbing her by the shoulders, every small fraction of tolerance fading from his eyes. 'Remember now you are my wife and, as such, will not only obey but respect me!'

Maxine glared up at him, her throat pounding with nervousness and fright, which she did her best to conceal with defiance. 'You might be able to make me obey you, but respect is another thing. You've done nothing so far to earn it, and never will, not as far as I'm concerned.'

He uttered a low laugh, wholly diabolical, his eyes glittering with a harsh fury as he drew her closer.

'What do I care for the respect of someone like you?'
he jeered. 'But there will be other things I do care about,
and I'm warning you, you'd better be prepared to be
generous, *mignonne*.'

CHAPTER SIX

As his mouth dropped to assault the jumping nerve at
the base of her throat, and his hands closed possessively
over the curving slimness of her hips, Maxine quivered
at his touch. She could feel the warmth of his lips lighting fires deep down in her treacherous body, and the
effort it took to push him away filled her with alarm.

Her eyes were wide as she backed from him. 'We can't
be properly married?' she gasped.

'We are properly married. At least, we soon will be,'
Kurt d'Estier mocked, his meaning inescapable, his
hard, good-looking face taunting.

He made no further attempt to touch her, yet despite
this she knew she was entirely at his mercy. She would
never, however, give in to him willingly. 'You put
something in my drink!' she cried, clinging to anger
like an armour.

'A few harmless herbs,' he agreed cynically. 'Otherwise you might have embarrassed the priest with your
raving and ranting. I seem to recall you have quite a
vocabulary, when you get started.'

He was referring to Mrs Martin's real daughter, so
ignoring what he said, Maxine rushed on, desperate to
find a way out of the mess she was in, 'We can't be
properly married in the eyes of your people. I've read
about Berber weddings.'

The quality of his grim smile told her he was well aware of her desire to escape him. 'I am not a true Berber, *ma chérie*, as I've already explained, although I do have their blood in my veins. But because they consider me one of them, I will one day take you back to the desert and introduce you to these good people as my wife. If you had been an innocent young girl we might even have been married there. I did think about it, but I feared they might have detected that you are not all you should be, and have been insulted.'

'That you didn't offer them the best, you mean?' Maxine's cheeks were scarlet.

'Something like that,' his firm mouth twisted as he watched her closely. 'They have a deep-rooted belief that only the pure and unsullied is good enough for me. But do not alarm yourself, *petite*. All things considered, I am well satisfied with what I've got. My fiancée was descended from the old French nobility, but as a considerable heiress you will do much to help my injured pride. My friends won't be so quick to mock when I produce you.'

Maxine felt her hot cheeks pale to coldness. What his friends thought didn't concern her, nor, she suspected, did their opinions bother him. It was what he would do to her when they met Mrs Martin and he discovered he had married her secretary, not her daughter, which almost stopped Maxine's heart in terror. Quaking, she contemplated Kurt's anger. He might have brought this all on himself by refusing to listen, but had she been firm enough? Guilt surged painfully as doubt consumed her, curling her hands into agitated fists which she laid on her fast beating breast.

From a distance she heard Kurt saying abruptly, 'Vega is here, Maxine. You will be glad to rest, and I have a great deal to see to. Later Vega will help you to dress and we will dine together.'

As Maxine followed the serving girl upstairs, she

wondered what 'a great deal to see to' entailed. Did he intend getting in touch with Mrs Martin? How long would it be before he told her of his marriage? He had given no hint as to whether Mrs Martin knew of her son's death or not? She bit her lip anxiously, feeling she ought not to have forgotten to ask about that. Being married in such a hurry, so unexpectedly, had put everything else from her mind. Mrs Martin would take it badly and she should have been there to help.

Nervously, Maxine's thoughts veered. What did Kurt intend doing with her? As in the desert, there was nowhere she could run to. Here it wasn't so much the sand as the high mountain peaks. Up to twelve thousand feet, they shimmered with dry heat under immense blue skies, like huge stone fortresses, tumbling down on to the plateaux where other frightening heights stretched out to meet them. There was no way she could find her way out as the route they had come by was twisting and tortuous. A prisoner she was and one she would undoubtedly remain until they returned to civilisation.

Kurt, she sensed, was attracted to her, but she would be a fool to imagine he loved her. As for herself, Maxine shivered, uneasily aware that if she were to examine her heart thoroughly she might find she was far more deeply involved than she cared to think about. When Kurt kissed her their lips clung, as if some potent chemistry was working between them, but it wouldn't be sensible to call this love. Lust might be more like it, she confessed to herself shamefacedly, conscious that until meeting Kurt d'Estier she hadn't known what it was to long, even vaguely, for a man to make love to her.

As Vega, with beaming smiles, ran her bath, Maxine sank listlessly into a chair, forcing herself to examine the situation without breaking down. Not for the first time she felt grateful for the strictness of convent life, which eliminated any tendency to wallow in self-pity. Staunchly she put aside the urgent desire to weep by biting her lip until it almost bled. In all probability, Kurt wouldn't be convinced she wasn't Mrs Martin's daughter until they reached England and Mrs Martin told him so herself. Confronted by Mrs Martin, and perhaps her real daughter, he would be left with no other option but to believe. What would he do then? Divorce was the most likely solution, but she wasn't sure. His religion must preclude this although she guessed there were ways—if one had as much influence as Kurt d'Estier. But until he met Mrs Martin he wasn't going to listen to Maxine's story, and she contemplated days, maybe weeks of having to listen to him expressing sardonic satisfaction with a situation which simply didn't exist.

Maxine might be young, but she suddenly felt twice her age. She might be innocent, but she was no fool. No one having eyes and ears in their head could remain ignorant these days, not about the facts of life. Not for a moment did Maxine doubt that Kurt meant to present Mrs Martin with a real marriage, possibly a pregnant wife. This, she admitted truthfully, if with an inward tremor, might not have been so terrible, not the way she felt about him; it was the thought of his fury when he discovered the truth which brought beads of perspiration to her brow. Even the thought of it made her feel ill. When this happened she had no illusions as to what her life would be afterwards, whether he succeeded in divorcing her or not.

After she had bathed she lay down on the wide bed and tried to relax. At once she realised this was impossible; her head ached and the muscles at the back of her neck were so tense she could have cried.

Vega, seeing her white face, was all concern. Before Maxine could protest she had turned her over and began gently massaging her shoulders and back. Lying on her stomach, Maxine forced herself to endure, hoping that it would at least stop her from thinking wholly of Kurt and perhaps going mad. Hadn't she heard there was magic in the fingers of these women of the East, born of centuries of yearning to please their men? It must have been remarkably effective magic as in a very short time she fell asleep.

When she woke, Vega helped her dress. Holding on to the numb submissiveness which still gripped her from Vega's soothing administrations, she allowed the girl to drape a swirling transparent skirt around her hips and a brief matching top over her shoulders. Her midriff was bare and she fancied she had the look of a dancing girl, dressed and perfumed, glinting with star-spangled embellishments which glittered in all the right places. Even her hair Vega brushed until it shone like a thick skein of pale yellow silk under the fine, silky veil she threw lightly across it. The longing for one of her own more conventional dresses faded as Maxine stared at herself, faintly intrigued. In the mirror she saw a beautiful stranger reflected, a young girl no longer but a woman, lovely enough to attract the attention of even a man such as Kurt d'Estier. She must be mistaken, it could only be a trick of the light, and Kurt d'Estier was too experienced a man to be taken in by a little superficial glamour. With a defeated sigh Maxine turned away to follow Vega downstairs.

To her surprise Kurt was waiting for her, a slight smile on his sensuous mouth, as though he congratulated himself on bringing his bride quickly to heel. All Maxine's protective numbness disappeared as he relieved her of the velvet caftan which Vega had slipped around her shoulders before leaving the bedroom.

If he appeared to tense slightly at the sight of her, he quickly recovered. She even discovered a hint of amusement, or thought she did, at the back of his eyes.

'Vega certainly has surpassed herself this evening,' his glance rested on the satin smooth skin at Maxine's waist. Touching it with an experimental finger, he asked mockingly, 'Is it like this all over?'

A flush came slowly up Maxine's neck. Under his cool, searching gaze she felt the heat of it scorching her face, making her heart race. Quickly she sat down as the servants brought in their dinner. 'I'm not allowed my own clothes, but if I was, I can assure you I wouldn't be wearing this.' She flicked a hand scornfully to her flimsy skirt, 'You might remember this before you start thinking I've dressed up for your benefit.'

His eyes glinted and, as she looked at him, Maxine's breath caught, in spite of herself, at his virile handsomeness. He was tall and bronzed, his shoulders broad and powerful beneath the loose white djellaba he wore. Curiously she wondered what he would look like in a European suit, but guessed he might be just as attractive. He would only have to flick his fingers to have women running.

Finding the thought oddly disquieting, she lowered her head as he sat down beside her so that her eyes might not give her away. For distraction she began to eat and was surprised to find she was hungry. As on her first night here she had scarcely eaten all day and felt almost ashamed of her appetite. It was as if her healthy young body refused to do without that which her mind would deny it.

Replete at last, she found she couldn't manage the delectable sweetmeats which were set before them. She only wanted a cup of coffee.

After filling her cup, Kurt said suavely, 'If you make love as well as you eat, *chérie*, I shall be more than satisfied.'

Flinching from what she considered crudeness, Maxine replied stiffly, 'I don't always eat so much. I was hungry.'

'This I realise,' he paused, his eyes reflective on her pink cheeks. 'None the less, I feel we might deal well together, you and I, especially since we have discovered we are not altogether incompatible. We are alone here, we might be wiser to enjoy the next few days, or weeks, rather than waste them in fruitless argument.'

Her voice came with difficulty through a decided agitation. 'And when we get back to civilisation?'

'When we get back to civilisation, as you put it, I don't think we need disrupt our respective lives too much, Maxine.'

Maxine couldn't keep the sharpness from her voice, although she knew he thought he was speaking to another girl. 'You mean I can do as I wish, you won't care?'

'That wasn't quite what I meant,' he retorted coldly. 'As my wife you will find you have a certain position to uphold, and you will act circumspectly, but I won't require your help in any part of the business. I have various residences, both here and in France. You might amuse yourself by devoting some attention to these.'

'Confine myself to the domestic side of things, you mean?' Maxine, in bitter indignation, quite forgot that once Kurt was convinced of her true identity he wouldn't be asking her to devote herself to anything!

He sighed impatiently. 'You will feel happier if you resign yourself, *ma chère*. I imagine, by the time we leave here, our brief interest in each other will have exhausted itself. It might help if you keep in mind how your brother repaid me for all I did for him, and resolve to make some recompense for his sins.'

Something of what he said hurt so much she had to retaliate. 'He couldn't force your fiancée into doing what she did.'

He smiled indifferently. 'How can we tell? Nor will we ever know, now. It is sufficient for me that I have you and that things have turned out tolerably well. I have a wife who is not unattractive, and through whom I will greatly benefit in the way of business. One, moreover, who need not trouble my conscience, should I decide to have an evening out with a woman friend.'

So this was what he meant when he talked of not disrupting his life! Maxine's breath caught and hurt in her throat. Yet how could she object when, from every angle, their marriage was a charade. If he intended acting it out it might be wiser to try appealing to the better side of him. She was sure he had one.

Controlling her painful reactions to his last remark, she looked at him entreatingly. 'We don't even know each other, not properly, Kurt, and you've just lost your *fiancée*.'

'What are you trying to say?' he drawled.

'That I understand, for all you like to tease me, that this marriage is only to be a business affair. That you are still in mourning, and you don't love me.'

His mouth twisted cynically. 'I lost my fiancée before she was ever killed, Maxine, and you never had a great regard for your brother, or your mother, despite your recent exaggerated concern. I don't believe either of us has any sincere mourning to do.'

'You are heartless!'

'Better to be so than a hypocrite, pretending to be heartbroken,' he sneered. 'As for our marriage being a business affair, you are quite right, it is, but I certainly intend taking it seriously. As long as I have you, my dear, your mother is going to suffer, as she'll never know whether you married me willingly or not. I recall she was quite obsessive over her son and daughter.'

Unable to endure any more, Maxine jumped to her feet. 'If you'll excuse me, I'm tired. I—I think I'll go to bed.'

His brief laugh smote her. 'I thought you wouldn't be able to wait much longer.'

'Wait much longer? I don't understand. You can't mean——?' Horrified, she broke off, staring at him.

His eyes glinted with something indefinable as he rose to tower over her. 'If you imagine our marriage isn't going to be a proper one, then you're mistaken. I don't intend leaving you an easy way out.'

Panic-stricken at his words, she turned to leave him, but was caught, pulled back to him, her cry of despair smothered against his lips as he kissed her bruisingly. When he took his mouth away she was shivering, fast in the merciless grip of something much stronger than herself.

'You understand?' His fingers under her chin turned her face towards him, so he could take his fill of her trembling mouth.

'God, you're a beast! You're cruel....' She scarcely heard what she was saying through the hammering of her heart as she gazed up at him, into the dark glitter of his eyes.

His face was grim as he released her, thrusting her almost impatiently from him. 'Stop trying to act the injured innocent, Maxine. It might help if you were to remember we are married, a status of respectability which you've never had before. And marriage to me can't be all that tragic, surely?'

'It could be,' she whispered, thinking of the future.

'You aren't totally indifferent to me.' His eyes rested with satisfaction on her palpitating breast.

Maxine's head dropped. How could she deny the way he made her feel, when his hands touched her body and his intolerant mouth plundered the soft redness of her own? She was ashamed of her complete response to his ruthless masculinity, but kisses were one thing. She couldn't bear to think what it would be like if he went any further.

She heard Kurt taunting, 'You must realise that while you might be able to cleverly disguise your true age, the years must soon catch up with you. Your chances of finding the right kind of husband can only get more remote, and, I repeat, we might yet do well together. In fact, *chérie*, I find myself quite looking forward to my wedding night.'

His harsh laughter, low though it was, followed Maxine as she fled from the room. All the way to her bedroom she felt that the devil was after her, and an inescapable fear lent wings to her feet.

In her room Vega waited, obviously eager to help prepare her new mistress for the pleasure of her lord and master, but Maxine quickly dismissed her, uncaring for once for the hurt expression on the girl's face. Stubbornly Vega hesitated. It was not until Maxine rather desperately assured her that she would explain to Kurt that the girl reluctantly departed.

When Vega had gone, Maxine sank down weakly on a chair, her mind curiously dull when she wanted to think clearly. If only Kurt had been kinder! Already she was more than a little in love with him. Perhaps it was foolish to try measuring emotion, but she did not know why, when he was near, she had often an urgent desire to be in his arms, and during the few times he had been away from her, she had been beset by all kinds of anxieties. That he had no real tenderness for her might have been hard enough to bear, but that he had married her merely to ensure revenge and further his business interests made her want to cry out with pain. It also made her aware of her incredible foolishness in allowing herself to care for him in the first place.

How long she sat there torn by nervous uncertainty, she couldn't tell, but she felt shock plunge through her afresh as the door pushed open and Kurt strode in. It was as if she had just learnt of his intentions, so startled was she.

His strong mouth tightening arrogantly, he stared at her, and no less intently she returned his regard, though her own eyes widened against the narrowed impatience in his. 'Aren't you ready for bed yet? Where's Vega? I told her to help you.'

He might truly have been a desert sheik, so used did he sound to having his every order obeyed. Maxine tried to look away from him but couldn't. He wore a loose kind of robe, but different from that which he had worn at dinner. This had a sash which tied around his broad but lean waist, and she had a shaken feeling it was more of a dressing gown and that he had nothing on underneath. He was hard, determined, totally without feeling, and she knew suddenly that up until this moment she hadn't taken him altogether seriously.

'I sent her away,' she said, trying to hide a mounting fear with sullen defiance. 'I refuse to be dressed and undressed like a child.'

'Whether you like it or not, you will conform,' there was menacing softness in his well-bred voice. 'From now on, *chérie*, you will do exactly as you are told.'

'No!'

In an instant he was beside her, pulling her to her feet. She heard his teeth snap. 'Your first lesson is not to disobey me. When my temper is aroused you will find me a dangerous man to cross.'

'Let me go!' She beat at him with small clenched fists.

She might have been pelting him with paper pellets for all the notice he took. He caught her hands in one of his, holding them easily against the hardness of his chest. 'If you refuse to have Vega undress you and won't do it yourself, then I must.' He sighed, his eyes resting with a kind of sardonic tolerance on her apprehensive face. 'If it amuses you, *ma chère*, to play the innocent bride, then it appears I must humour you in some ways.'

'Don't touch me!'

His laughter was insolent as he released her wrists and his arms went around her. 'I might not, if I hadn't discovered a liking for touching you, and you hadn't been my wife. Or if I could believe you were really mourning Colin. Are you?'

She couldn't lie about this. As his arms tightened she trembled but shook her head. Colin Martin had been almost a stranger. So, too, was this man who held her so closely, yet Kurt made her heart race as no other man had ever done.

As his hands slid over her slender back she tried to wrench away. This must have been a mistake, as it appeared to incense him. Relentlessly his mouth closed over hers, remorselessly sensuous. Maxine felt within her trembling body a frightening, primitive reaction. Her blood quickened as his hold imprisoned her and his mouth began exploring hers deeply. His arms held her, bending her backwards, slightly away from him, to give him freer access to the softness of her breasts. He moved quickly, impatient of her clothes, and took a savage hold of her bodice, as if prepared to rip.

'No!' Desperation lending her strength, Maxine choked and spluttered as she pushed away from him. The blood rushed through her head. Before her self-control went completely she must do something. If he had loved her how different it might have been! 'Please, Kurt,' she entreated, 'I would rather undress myself, if you would leave me for ten minutes?'

'Mon dieu!' His voice thickening with anger, he made no attempt to do as she asked. He stared at her intently, looking through the uncertainty and fright at what seemed very much like passion at the back of her shadowed eyes. 'I don't intend leaving you for even ten seconds,' he assured her. 'Come, sweetheart,' he jeered savagely, 'it is years ago, but I remember how the man you were with was taking your clothes off, and you were almost purring. You would surely grant your husband the same privilege? To see your lovely body is something you can't deny me. If you are sensible, chérie, I will be kind. But I won't promise anything if you continue to defy me.'

'No...!'

Taking no notice, he began unfastening the silver buttons at her throat with deliberate fingers. His knuckles pressed into her skin. She felt the flames from their contact licking through her, melting her resistance. Too shaken to move, she felt the brush of his mouth on the shadowed cleft between her breasts, as he slid the silken cloth from her shoulders.

'I had forgotten,' he said huskily, 'just how beautiful you are.'

'Kurt, you don't understand!' she groaned, her senses beginning to swim as he demanded surrender. She could feel the hardness of his strong thighs against hers, as he made no effort to disguise his growing desire.

Suddenly, with a strength normally beyond her, she jerked quickly away from him. As she turned to escape him, she caught his face, her nails ripping his deeply tanned skin and drawing blood. With a frightened gasp she saw what she had done, but didn't stop. Taking him by surprise, she rushed to the door, as his hand jumped to his cheek. But like an animal, the loss of his defence was only momentary. His reflex was that of the desert tiger, instantaneous, and just as merciless.

He caught at her hair, flying long and thickly behind her, as she ran in wild panic. Grasping it with what seemed intentional cruelty, he halted her headlong flight from the room. His face set in lines of harsh anger, he hauled her back against him until she cried for mercy.

'Why should I stop hurting you?' His voice was cold as he released her hair, only to trap her in his arms.

His fury was aroused, and Maxine, feeling bitter tears sting her eyes, realised she had gone about things in the worst possible way. Taking no notice of her wet cheeks, he twisted her head on his broad shoulder and took her mouth—in a kiss designed wholly to humiliate.

'You'll be sorry, Kurt,' she wept, when minutes later he was staring at her bruised lips.

'I intend teaching you to be sorry, you little wildcat,' he retorted harshly, his hold on her trembling body not lessening an inch. 'I am a man, and I'll have an obedient wife. Your little games no longer amuse me, I am tired of them. I am also impatient, *petite*.'

'Give me time, Kurt.'

'That is something I won't give you.' His mouth dropped against the fluttering pulse in her throat. His lips were insistent, as though he hungered for her, although he took them away to study her fluctuating colour. 'Before you leave here there must be no question of your ever being able to escape me, *mignonne*. You understand?'

'No!' Maxine's protesting cry was almost a scream. Yet deep within her something jerked and moved, responding to his primitive threat as if her body had a will of its own. Her voice cried a denial, while all the strength left her limbs.

'But yes.' He kissed her now, with an expertise which left her reeling. Her legs gave way under her as he picked her up and carried her to the bed. There he removed the last of her clothing, his hands catching her roughly as he did so, stirring flickers of response that disturbed her terribly.

'Stop fighting me,' he ordered curtly, his eyes smouldering darkly, as he looked down on her bare limbs. 'Let us at least get some pleasure out of our unwanted alliance. As a woman of considerable experience, Maxine, you must know how to please a man. How to give a little satisfaction, as well as receive it. Come, let us enjoy what we can, while we can.'

As he lay down beside her she felt his mouth exploring her face, the soft skin of her cheeks and throat. When she went rigid he bit the small pink lobe of her ear quite painfully and ran a taunting hand over her shoulders and breast. She couldn't open her heavy eyes when she heard him fling his robe to the floor, but she felt his nakedness as he crushed her against him.

In one last desperate attempt to be free of him, her fingers wrenched at his hair as he forced her beneath his powerful body, but as his mouth returned to hers, her own opened on an uncontrollable little gasp as she was swept by a sensuous surge of feeling.

As her arms went up around his shoulders, and her hands curved tightly on the nape of his neck, she felt the triumphant laughter moving softly through him. Yet a full surge of impossible longing heated her blood to molten desire, as his hold tightened, and she surrendered helplessly.

'That's better,' he murmured against her mouth, his voice deep with an arrogant satisfaction, as he felt her slim body stretching sensuously up to him.

For Maxine everything but the man who held her so passionately was fading. She could feel the beat of his heart, the heat of his skin, and potent nerves began fluttering in the depth of her stomach. Clinging to him, her lips parted, she submitted to his demands. She felt him groan, and knew she must be arousing him to the same urgency they both seemed to share. He made love to her until ripples of sensation darted through her body and she felt so weak she was unable to utter one word of protest as he did what he liked with her.

His weight pinned her, making her aware of his impatience, but for all she knew he expected to find her experienced she wasn't prepared for the unleashed savageness of his desire. He thought her a woman who had known many lovers, but because she hadn't even had one she hadn't quite realised what this might mean. The feel of her soft body yielding at last appeared to shatter what was left of his self-control.

He crushed her devouringly, his practised lovemaking awakening her to heights of dark desire, while the skilful pressures of his muscular body removed all her strength. Her hands left the back of his head to dig frantically into the hard muscles of his shoulders, moving backwards and forwards with a mounting urgency.

The damp warmth of his mouth tortured her, and his

breath dragged deep. 'I've wanted you since I met you again, and you can't deny you want me. I can feel your heart beating right through me, *chérie*.'

When he took her for a moment everything went blank, a moment of total shock, almost annihilating the burning wantoness inside her. Like a small, desperate animal she flung her arms back across the pillows, shrinking convulsively away from him. She heard him rasp something guttural in French, then from a thick layer of excruciating fog she felt him pause. If he had been angry before, a fresh fury appeared to shake him, but whatever the cause, it wasn't strong enough at this late hour to conquer his searing desire.

His passion overwhelmed her as pain gave way swiftly to something else, something which had her clinging to him once more and swept her into total abandonment. She seemed to dissolve before an electrical storm of sensation which was so intense as to make her cry out. There was no escape, nor did she seek to find any, as the purely physical took over, merging body and mind until the whole world seemed to explode in her face.

Afterwards, as he rolled away from her, she lay dazed, only slowly becoming conscious that, while she hurt, she had experienced something else, something more devastating yet wonderful than she had ever dreamt possible.

Her hands felt numb as she groped to rub the tears from her hot cheeks. Some fell saltily on her unsteady mouth, making her flinch. Her lips were sore, bruised from Kurt's hard kisses. 'Darling,' she murmured weakly, not wholly conscious of what she was saying, her arms reaching out, longing to have him holding her again. In spite of the agony she had endured she had also seemed to catch a glimpse of heaven.

'Kurt?' she repeated, the eyes she turned to him huge with half pleading uncertainty, her former enmity forgotten.

It took her several seconds to understand that his withdrawal and silence was not of remorse but of anger. A black fury held him and, if he partly controlled it, it blazed unmistakably from his face, denying the primitive passion which had been there only moments ago.

Picking up his robe from the floor, he pulled it savagely around his wide, naked shoulders. As he loomed over her again, his jaw was rigid with menace and he had no pity at all for her trembling bewilderment. 'Who are you?' he asked roughly, as though she was a complete stranger.

Who am I? The question went round and round in Maxine's head, making no sense whatsoever. 'I suppose —I mean, I thought I was your wife ...'

'Fool!' he rasped. 'I want to know who you really are. I realise now you aren't Mrs Martin's daughter.' His eyes glittering with an unholy rage, he suddenly reached down and took hold of her. His hands closed over her pale shoulders and he shook her until her head rolled helplessly on her slender neck and her whimper of pain became a sob.

'I told you,' she wept, 'but you refused to believe....'

'You told me!' Kurt's anger didn't diminish, Maxine's white face apparently moving him not one bit. 'You told me after you had been here some time, but not before. Initially you made no clear effort to correct my belief that you were Colin Martin's sister.'

'Mrs Martin asked me not to.'

'Why not, in God's name?'

'Because she wanted you to think she had sent someone of real importance,' Maxine whispered, finding it difficult, before his terrible fury to speak at all.

'And you were fool enough to agree, but clever enough just to enlighten me enough to make me believe you were putting on an act.'

Her arms felt sore and bruised like the rest of her, but he didn't release his relentless grasp. Maxine felt sick with misery and very unsure of herself. How could she answer him? Momentarily she closed her eyes, attempting to shut out the hatred she could see as he stared at her. She had, she supposed, with Mrs Martin's warnings and pleading in mind, been anything but clear, to begin with anyway, as to her true identity. She must have been guilty of deception in a way, yet hadn't she done all she possibly could to convince him of the truth in the end?

Feeling in a greater muddle than ever, she said unhappily, 'Mrs Martin only intended that I should bring you a message of sympathy. I know she never dreamt I would have to go further than Casablanca, and she thought I would only be seeing you for a very short time.'

'She didn't hope to deceive me, I suppose? She didn't hope that I would console myself with you, and that by the time I discovered the truth my anger would have died down?'

The words were bitten off with such cold anger that Maxine shook. 'I—I couldn't tell you if this was her intention, but I'm sure it was not. You must realise she was distraught.'

'Sacré dieu!' suddenly he thrust Maxine away from him, seeing the nakedness which, in her distress, she had forgotten. 'Cover yourself, you little tramp. Don't ever let me see you like this again.' Reaching for a crumpled sheet he flung it over her, waiting while she pulled it numbly up to her chin before continuing his attack. All their shared passion was forgotten, the desire he had felt for her, Maxine could see, had turned to hate. A hatred impaled firmly on his dark, unforgiving face.

CHAPTER SEVEN

COLD with humiliation, Maxine whispered, 'I expect you'll try to get a divorce?'

'Yes,' she saw his nostrils tense savagely with resolve, 'I certainly will arrange something, but not in the near future. Do you wish people to laugh at me again? First I allow my fiancée to run off with another man, then I am fooled into marrying the wrong girl. *Dieu*, when I realised that you had never known a man I could have killed you! How did you expect to get away with it, I wonder?'

'I didn't know,' she replied painfully, colour surging to her white cheeks as her eyes fell on the ruined bed. 'Perhaps if I had,' she added, with bitter frankness, 'I might have invited you to find out, before we were married.'

Her tortured irony passed unnoticed as the dark blue of his eyes chilled like Arctic seas. 'More fool me,' he grated. 'I might have known such a look of youthfulness couldn't be faked. Yet not even when Vega assured me that your fair hair was genuine was I convinced.' Vindictively he stared at the tears Maxine was trying hard to control, without compassion for the traumatic experience she had just gone through. 'You are, of course, of good family? Your parents?'

'Both dead.'

No word of sympathy, only a curious pause. 'Where, then, were you brought up?'

Did it matter? Maxine wondered hysterically. 'In a home. At least. . . .'

'*Mon dieu!*' furiously she was cut off and the look he flung at her made her actually cringe away from him. 'An orphan from a children's home! A nobody, and I had to marry you. I couldn't have done worse if I'd searched the back streets of Casablanca.'

White to the lips, Maxine cried, 'An orphan is as much a human being as anyone else, Kurt, and just as much in need of understanding and sympathy.'

As soon as the words were out, she wished she hadn't added that last bit, it sounded too much like pleading. She need not have worried as his face closed against her completely. His hand came out to grasp her arm so painfully it brought fresh tears to her eyes. 'Do not weary me, *madame*. Your defence of your kind may be admirable, but I did not want one of you for my wife.'

She didn't know what to say to this as she realised his upbringing would have taught him to put most other considerations before love. Yet surely he couldn't have been so bothered about his fiancée if he hadn't loved her?

'Have you any money of your own?' he snarled.

Would this have improved matters? Wishing futilely that she might have been a millionairess, if only for the pleasure of flinging it in his arrogant face, Maxine clenched her hands unhappily. 'No—I'm sorry, Kurt.'

'God!' his voice was as cutting as steel, 'so I'm tied to a lowborn, penniless nobody.' His hands slid up her arms to her shoulders and tightened menacingly. 'But do not worry,' he said thickly, 'the joke will be on you. I will make you suffer, my young impostor, as you've never suffered in your life!'

Helplessly Maxine stared up at him, almost oblivious of his painful grip. He had been ruthless before, now he appeared more so. She could understand his pride had suffered a severe blow, as she was indeed a nobody, and his arrogance was such he would find it impossible to forgive her. Yet she couldn't forget the rapport they had shared, the moments when a mutual desire had bound them irrevocably together. When every touch of lips, breast and thighs had blazed with a kind of poetical magic, with an unbearable, mounting excitement which could surely never have been experienced by either one of them if the other hadn't reciprocated fully. She knew little about such physical matters, but it seemed they had known a rare kind of rapture.

'Tomorrow,' Kurt continued grimly, 'we will talk, you and I. By the morning my head will be clear and I will tell you exactly what I mean to do. But don't imagine you can escape me, Maxine. You will never do that until the day I choose to get rid of you.'

So saying, he thrust her back against her pillows, leaving her with such harshly contained fury in his face that she knew his reactions, on discovering the truth of her identity, had gone far beyond that which was usual in a man who considered himself deceived. For the first time in his life, perhaps, Kurt d'Estier's brilliant intelligence had let him down, and someone was to suffer. With a hollow feeling of utter misery, Maxine was aware that this someone could only be herself.

Contrary to her trembling expectations, Kurt didn't send for her next morning. Instead he sent a note with Vega, requesting her to be ready to leave for Casablanca before noon. Surprisingly the clothes she had come here in were returned. With Vega watching, Maxine put them on again, feeling, as she did so, that the period since she had last worn them was something she had dreamt. It had been evening when Vega had taken them away. Now it was morning. The days in between had all the frightening unreality of a nightmare.

Unfortunately, unlike a nightmare, what had happened during these last few days couldn't be so easily dismissed. Never again would she be the same innocent girl who had come so blindly to Morocco. Kurt had married her and then considered he had been tricked. His pride was suffering as he had discovered he had married a girl of no importance, a girl who would certainly never inherit Mrs Martin's considerable wealth, which would have proved a balm to the injustice her son had done him —a subtle form of revenge.

Kurt would never forgive her, and Maxine knew she was vulnerable enough where he was concerned to find such a punishment beyond enduring. Already, even after a sleepless night of lonely anguish, some treacherous part of her was longing to be back in his arms—arms which, on his sworn assurance, would never open to her again.

Dressed, she said goodbye to Vega, who gazed at her with puzzled eyes. She knew the girl couldn't understand why Kurt hadn't been near the bedroom all morning, and sensed that Vega wondered, from the rumpled state of the bed, how he had ever brought himself to leave it. Maxine was tempted to explain that there was no amour in Kurt's heart, but such a declaration would be both childish and futile. She thanked Vega wanly as she left the room, but that was all.

The girl bobbed a quaint little curtsy, which told Maxine clearly that she wasn't used to appreciation, and smiled. '*Au revoir, madame*,' she said, 'I will be here when you come again.'

Why did she sound so sure? Maxine sighed deeply as she walked away. Downstairs Kurt waited for her, though not in the same manner as he had done the previous evening. He came impatiently from the back of the hall, a stranger in a dark suit, impeccably cut, the jacket fitting his broad shoulders in a way only achieved by the very best tailoring. With it he wore a white shirt which contrasted effectively with his deep tan. Looking at him, she felt slightly stunned yet oddly grateful. He might have been any well-groomed business man from any European city. This morning his good looks blended with a suave sophistication which made Maxine feel naïve in the extreme. Without his haik and white burnous he was something of a stranger, but she felt grate-

ful that in some way this seemed to help her keep a
tighter rein over her unsteady emotions.

This morning his eyes were hard, the coldness on his
face even repelling as he looked at her. 'Good morning,'
he said formally, as if she had merely been a casual
acquaintance who had spent the night, although she
doubted if he would ever look at such a person with such
dislike. 'We leave by truck, but a helicopter will pick
us up after we clear the mountains. We should be in
Casablanca by nightfall.' He offered no other explanation.

If he noticed Maxine's paleness, her deeply shadowed
eyes, he took no notice. Earlier she had felt relieved
that he had decided not to talk, but now she felt an
urge for some kind of communication with him. Surely
something could be dredged out of the ashes of their
marriage? There must be some way of redeeming something before the fire went out completely? She didn't
know why she wanted to save anything, but there was
inside her a sudden urgency.

'Kurt!' she cried, as he turned away. And, as he
paused, she entreated, 'Couldn't we—we talk things
over?'

'*Madame*,' he said curtly, his eyes cruelly critical on
her ravaged face, finding her so plain as to be uninteresting, 'I was wrong last night. There is nothing to
talk about. There are a few instructions I will give you
in Casablanca, but there is nothing else I wish to discuss.'

Still she tried, lowering her head so he wouldn't see
the glimmer of tears. 'We must have something to say
to each other, Kurt?'

'You are mistaken, *madame*.' His deep voice was
smooth. 'From now on we are strangers, even though for
a while we must live in the same house. I have no use for
a woman who lives by her wits.'

'No, Kurt ...' in agony she stared at him beseechingly,
'you've got it all wrong!'

They were alone. Izaac was outside, talking to the

truck driver, so Kurt didn't bother to lower his voice. 'You kept your body and sold it to the highest bidder, but if a buyer doesn't happen to like what he has bought then he is at liberty to throw such goods out of the window—out of his life. That, *madame*, is what is going to happen to you, eventually. In the meantime,' he paused, running his eyes over her insolently, 'do not come running to me begging for love. You would simply be wasting your time.'

The journey to Casablanca didn't take too long, but for Maxine the hours were interminable. She was frightened and this didn't help her to think clearly, to devise a plan which might enable her to escape Kurt, and the immediate fate he was planning for her. By the time they reached Casablanca she felt ill, and something about her must have warned him she wouldn't be able to hold out much longer. Without hesitation, at the airport, he thrust her straight into his waiting car and drove her to his flat.

His flat astonished her, as had all his homes in turn. This one, set in a sprawling department block, was large, ultra-modern and luxurious, such a complete contrast to the ksar and his desert tents that she could only stare numbly. Mrs Martin had taught her quite a lot about antiques and although the flat was modern, Maxine thought she recognised one or two choice pieces. There was a charming gilt *canapé*, upholstered in gold silk, and an enchanting small French *bonheur du jour* with a French clock incorporated within the top, and at the other side of the hall, a really superb nineteenth-century French bureau *plat* on cabriole supports. Mrs Martin had one very like it. There were other elegant pieces she didn't recognise and she found she could no longer concentrate. Perhaps Kurt would tell her about them some time.

From the hall Kurt indicated a long passage. 'The bedrooms are over there. You can choose which one you like, apart from mine, which is on the end. You can scarcely expect me to accommodate you there.'

Would he have done if she had been Mrs Martin's daughter? Accepting the cool drink he put in her hands almost reluctantly, Maxine stood, nervously undecided. Did he expect her to choose now? She had a discouraging picture of herself inspecting each room, weighing each one up. She didn't want to stay here at all. Already, in spite of the luxury and comfort, the flat felt like a prison.

To put off the moment of decision, she glanced at Kurt as he stood watching her closely. 'I didn't bring many clothes. Just what I'm wearing, actually, apart from one long dress.'

'What is that supposed to convey?' he asked with terse impatience, as if he had other, more important things to see to.

Again she was shattered by his coldness and had to fight with the lump in her throat. 'Just that I can't spend all my time in one dress.'

'No one expects you to,' he asserted coolly. 'I will get my secretary to open accounts for you in some of the larger stores, and if we go to Paris you can choose what you like there. You will not lack for material things, *madame*.'

Why did he keep calling her that? And did he really think material things mattered so much to a woman when he deprived her of—of other things? He was so distant, it was difficult to believe he was the same man who had made passionate love to her only hours ago. She averted her suddenly flushed face lest he should guess her thoughts. 'I could collect what I have from the hotel where I stayed, in the morning, and you don't have to open any accounts for me. I still have enough money to buy a few clothes.'

His eyes blazed as he came nearer, taking her shoulders, in what seemed his favourite act of cruelty. 'While you are my wife, in the eyes of the world, you will wear only what I provide. I do not wish my wife to be seen in cheap rags. As for your things, I had your case removed from your hotel several days ago. You will find it here somewhere.'

Again she felt his breath on her face, but it was cool, with no hint of passion unless it was anger. His eyes did hold a hint of interest, but it too was without warmth as he surveyed the bruised look of her mouth, the darker shadows of bruising on her throat, where his mouth had exerted pressure when she had tried to resist him.

As she shrank back he smiled caustically. 'Do not be afraid, Maxine, I have no intention of slaking my thirst at the moment. If I feel like pandering to my male needs and there is no one else available, we might come to some arrangement.'

Maxine's hand shot out, before she could prevent it, in a wholly primitive attempt to strike him. The humility which had kept her submissive all day dissolved in a surge of hate which sought some definite outlet.

Catching her hand before it could do any damage, he held it tightly. A dull flush mounted his hard cheeks and he looked as if he would have liked to have broken her in two. So convincing was this impression that she was trembling convulsively when behind them there came a slight cough and a woman appeared.

Glancing at Maxine curiously, she spoke to Kurt in the rapid French Maxine found almost impossible to follow. She could only make out, as Kurt released her, that someone had been trying to contact him urgently, and might call later.

After replying, Kurt introduced Maxine. 'This is my wife.'

If the woman was startled she quickly suppressed her surprise, but it returned again to her rounded eyes when

Kurt explained briefly that he and Maxine had been married the day before.

'Madame Lange comes in each day and looks after the flat,' he said, ignoring both the woman's obvious astonishment and Maxine's discomfort.

Maxine could think of nothing to say. She could only wonder what she was going to find to do all day if Madame Lange did all the work.

Madame Lange, removing her eyes with apparent difficulty from Maxine's strained face, asked Kurt if he would be requiring dinner as usual, at eight.

'Yes,' he replied. 'And as we may have a guest you had better lay another place, just in case.'

Unable to arouse any interest in the expected guest, as soon as the woman had gone, Maxine asked if she could go to her room. If someone was coming to see Kurt, he might prefer to see them alone. Even if he requested her to be present she felt she couldn't face anyone until she felt better.

Before he spoke he looked as if he was deep in thought, but he turned to her immediately. 'I told you,' he said curtly, 'to choose your own. You'll probably find your suitcase in one, if that's any help.'

Maxine did find her case in one of them, the room next to Kurt's, down the passage. It was too near to him, but what did it matter? The way he thought of her, a few feet would be the same as a few hundred miles.

This bedroom, she was relieved to find, had its own bathroom, making it entirely self-contained. Bathing quickly, she lay on the bed, her legs weak from a terrible exhaustion. After doing nothing all day she couldn't be in need of rest, but she felt too dreadful to do anything else. Sobs shaking her slender body, she cried until she fell asleep. When she woke an hour later she took another shower and dressed.

The one long dress she had brought was uncrushable and came out of her suitcase ready to wear. In better shape than its owner! Maxine gave a mirthless giggle as she smoothed the silky material over her hips and adjusted the simple, rounded neckline. It wasn't a dress to impress anybody, least of all a man like Kurt, the husband who didn't want her. Uneasily she stared at her reflection in the mirror, well aware of what he would think.

Giving a deep sigh, she tried to do something about the tear stains on her face, but while make-up partly disguised them it didn't hide the young misery in her clouded grey eyes. It was only pride that drove her from her room to face whatever else the day might yet have in store for her.

Kurt said they would dine at eight and it was only half past seven, but Maxine knew if she didn't go now she might never make it. Going down the passage to the hall, she found herself hoping, cowardly, that Kurt might have gone out, yet dreading to find him not there. It was frightening to realise how she could scarcely bear to lose sight of him, despite his opinion of her.

He was in the lounge, which led straight off the hall—a modern room, without a fire, with deep chairs placed around its rug-strewn floor. Its appearance, though pleasing, was curiously impersonal. It contained knick-knacks, but nothing like the beautiful antiques in the hall. She liked the hall better.

When she came through the door Kurt stared at her as though he was contemplating another piece of furniture. 'If that's the sort of dress you favour then you can get rid of it. I'm not running an orphanage here.'

The colour ran painfully under Maxine's fair skin, but she pretended she hadn't heard him. 'Is that woman, Madame Lange, your housekeeper?'

His eyebrows rose, 'Is it so important?' Then, when Maxine didn't speak, 'Yes. She doesn't sleep here, but she does look after me. I suppose you could call her that.'

'You hadn't told her we were married?'

His mouth curled. 'There was scarcely time.'

'But she knew about your—your fiancée.'

Abruptly he answered, his voice chilly, 'Most people know about my fiancée, Maxine, but they will soon forget. Just as, one day, they'll forget about you.'

Again, while daggers plunged inside her, Maxine tried to take no notice. Unconsciously she drew nearer to him, looking up at him anxiously. 'If Madame Lange does all the work, Kurt, what will I do with myself all day?'

'Find some other way of amusing yourself.' His smile, as he took a deep drink of his whisky, was cruel. 'Usually, in France, a young wife enjoys preserving her energy for her husband's pleasure, but I'm afraid you might have to find another way of getting rid of yours.'

Although she lifted her chin, Maxine felt her face go scarlet. 'I'm afraid I don't care for that kind of talk,' she said primly.

'I can do better than that,' he jeered, suddenly pulling her close. Moulding her to him, before she could retreat, he lowered his head and his mouth crushed down on hers. His arms went around her, his hands so rough on her shoulders and waist that they hurt. Yet this didn't stop her from surrendering weakly, as through the very centre of her body a flood of warm feeling swept, making her come immediately alive. His face was dark with quickening passion, and the hardness of his mouth was arousing in her a kind of desperate delight.

Just as her arms began curving around his neck, he thrust her away. 'Kurt?' His kisses had made the room spin. When he put her from him she almost fell.

A pulse jerked at the side of his mouth, but his voice was low and mocking. 'Collect yourself, Maxine. Our guest will be here at any moment.'

She couldn't bear to be treated with such scornful indifference. How could he make love to her like this and expect her to remain undisturbed? Resentfully she cried, 'You promised never to kiss me again. I didn't ask you to, and it was more of a threat....'

'In the heat of the moment, perhaps I did,' his voice was silky, 'but there might be better forms of punishment than neglect. Frustration, for example. You say you hate me, but in my arms you seem to deny it.'

At this stage Madame Lange put her head around the door. She announced the visitor while Maxine sank gratefully into a chair, aghast at Kurt's astuteness.

'Miss Martin, *monsieur*.'

Miss Martin! In the act of brushing her rumpled hair from off her hot forehead, Maxine froze. It couldn't be! It would be too incredible! Mrs Martin's daughter was in Mexico. Mrs Martin hadn't even tried to get in touch with her, after they had heard about Colin.

'Maxine!' Hearing the warm recognition in Kurt's voice Maxine knew, without a shadow of doubt, this must indeed be Mrs Martin's daughter.

Slowly, as though it hurt, she turned her head to stare at the charming woman who swept towards Kurt, her hands outstretched. Maxine had never met her; she had only seen photographs of a girl who looked very like herself. The woman who bore down on them now did bear a slight resemblance, but that was all. In fact, Maxine realised, unless one looked for it, there just wasn't any.

This woman had Maxine's height, much the same shape of nose and grey eyes but little more. Her waist, which might have been slender at twenty, had thickened considerably, but if her figure was heavier it was so superbly gowned as to allow this to pass almost unnoticed. Her furs alone must have cost a small fortune.

Kurt took her hands. 'I seem to remember you were blonde last time we met,' he smiled.

'I've been in Mexico,' the woman smiled straight into his eyes as she shook her beautifully waved brown head. 'It wasn't convenient, where I was, to have it retinted.'

Her eyes swung past Kurt to rest on Maxine. For a moment she looked startled, then glancing back at Kurt, she exclaimed, 'That must be the girl who Mother says she sent? My double—or so Mother seems to think.'

'Something like what you used to be,' Kurt replied with smooth disparagement, 'when you were rather young and uninteresting. She even had the same name.'

'Had?'

'You're still as sharp, Maxine,' his eyes slid coolly over the woman whose hands he held flatteringly. 'Now she is Maxine d'Estier, my wife. We were married yesterday.'

'Married!' the other woman gasped.

'Don't look so startled, *chérie*,' he smiled. 'It might have been a mistake, but it is unfortunately true.'

'But why, Kurt?' Maxine, now cold all over, saw Mrs Martin's daughter gazing up at him imploringly. 'Mother only sent her to bring you a message. I was on my way.'

'Why ...!' Maxine sat up, but Kurt silenced her with a sharp look, wholly forbidding, before he turned to Colin's sister again, shrugging his broad shoulders regretfully. 'I'm afraid there has been misunderstandings all round, but nothing that a little time and patience can't put right. Now tell me, *ma chère*, are you here to stay?'

Before Maxine's anguished eyes, he led the woman over the room and gave her a drink. Then he proceeded to question her quietly as to why she was here, all the time gazing down at her, cosseting her as though she were someone very special.

A little while later, when he excused himself to have a word with Madame Lange about dinner, Mrs Martin's daughter swung around to Maxine vindictively. Gone was the purring softness she had shown Kurt. In its place was a spiteful anger.

'You little cheat!' she cried. 'I don't know what your

game is, but it's quite clear Kurt can't wait to get rid of you.'

Maxine felt so wounded and humiliated she couldn't think of a word to say. Kurt had as good as admitted their marriage was a mistake, so what would be the use of denying it?

'He must have thought, because you looked like me, that you would do,' the woman muttered. 'He would have married me years ago if I'd given him any encouragement.'

Half desperately, Maxine said, 'But you're married now.'

'No, I'm not. Did Kurt really think so? I could have been, of course, but I decided not to. I got back just after you left. I was tired of Mexico.'

'Then you know about Colin?'

'You don't have to whisper! Yes, I know, but why should I mourn? We never liked each other.'

'But your mother?'

'Oh, she'll get over it, especially as I've promised to be good and carry on with the family business. I've twice the brain Colin had. Kurt and I will work well together.'

'You don't mean to stay?'

'I definitely do, my girl. Hasn't Kurt just denied that you have a real marriage? I have no doubt he means to have it set aside, one way or another. In a few months, weeks maybe, I could be stepping into your shoes. Before that, unofficially. If you follow?' Maxine Martin sneered.

All through dinner, from which Kurt refused to let her escape, Maxine sat in a cold kind of daze. Mrs Martin's daughter—Max, as she apparently preferred to be called —reminded her of a ruthless predator, as unscrupulous as Kurt himself. Perhaps this was why they appeared to appreciate each other so much. She had attacked Maxine immediately, entirely viciously and to the point, then ignored her, as had Kurt. The two of them, with as little emotion as they might apply to a stranger, discussed Colin's death, how it would affect the various companies, the problems of the law which stated that Moroccans must hold the greatest number of shares. Kurt's position, though Maxine didn't completely understand it, seemed much more secure than Mrs Martin's, but as no one explained anything to her she was made to feel very much the odd man out—an impression which she gathered neither was reluctant to bestow on her.

Hollowly Maxine realised that though Colin's sister was hard and sophisticated, she was also attractive and intelligent, and that Kurt not only enjoyed talking to her but was not adverse to making discreet love to her, even with his wife looking on. This obviously didn't disturb him. He laid his hand on Max Martin's bare arm and smiled into her eyes as if his wife didn't exist. Much later, when Max rose to go and he said he would see her back to her hotel, Maxine felt quite ill as she met his coldly derisive glance. Yet, as well, she was aware of a faint relief that he hadn't insisted the woman stayed here with them.

She didn't see Kurt again until the next evening, after a day which she spent alone, without any knowledge of where he was or what he was doing. She rose early to find him already gone. He wasn't there and she couldn't help wondering if he had spent the night with Max at the hotel. When Madame Lange said he had had breakfast an hour ago, her heart lightened beyond what seemed sensible.

The curious exhaustion which she had known since leaving the ksar was still with her, but not even when Madame Lange suggested a walk might do her good did she go out. All day Maxine stayed in the flat, hoping Kurt would ring, but the telephone remained silent and time dragged dismally.

She had nothing to do but plenty to think about, and she would rather it had been more the other way around.

Or if she had had someone to share her worries they might not have hurt so much. She had no one to confide in and, for the first time in her life, was very aware of it. The shock of meeting Mrs Martin's daughter had been nothing to the unease she had known when Kurt had been so nice to the girl. Only now was she beginning to understand what it was like to be tied to a man who had nothing but revenge in his heart. First it had been against Colin, now his hatred had transferred to herself. Nothing mattered but that his wife should suffer and be got rid of.

At the ksar he had said if anyone was to discover he had been tricked into marrying Maxine, he would become an object of ridicule. Yet wouldn't Colin's sister demand an explanation as to why Kurt had married her mother's secretary so precipitately? Maxine wished she knew. There was nothing, she supposed, to stop her from going to Colin's sister herself and giving her the whole story. But she shrank from this, not eager to do anything which might hurt Kurt, regardless of how badly he treated her.

That night when he came, he strode into her bedroom without knocking. Having bathed but not dressed, she was just reaching for her hairbrush when she glanced up and saw him.

'Kurt?' Dropping the brush, she turned to him. Last night he had been immaculate but coldly unapproachable. Now he looked strained, his hair rumpled. There were lines around his mouth, too. Somehow she felt a quick compassion. 'You're tired?' she faltered.

He took the hairbrush from her. She had a fancy he would liked to have beaten her with it. 'Not so much tired,' he snapped, 'as wearied by my own foolishness.'

'Well, I wish you wouldn't look at me like that!' she cried, wondering how to bear his chilling stare. 'What have I done now?'

He went on staring at her, his eyes roaming moodily

over her fragile figure before returning to the faint tremble on the curve of her soft mouth, which belied the note of aggression in her voice. 'I wonder if you guessed,' he asked slowly, 'that when Colin and my late fiancée married, as they apparently did, she had already arranged to leave him all her money?'

'No,' she protested with sharp surprise, 'how could I?' Pausing suddenly, she realised what he was getting at. 'This must mean, then that Mrs Martin and her daughter will inherit it all, in the end?'

'Every penny,' he snarled.

'So ...' Maxine floundered, 'if you'd waited, and married the girl who really is Colin's sister ...?'

'Don't worry,' he bit off savagely, 'I will have it all in time. When a little time has passed and I am free of you.'

'Kurt,' she gulped, her face white, unable to believe he could be so mercenary but conscious that the French might consider such things important, 'I've told you before, you can't blame me completely for what happened.'

'Don't let me hear that again.' His long, lean fingers tensed on the brush he still held.

Maxine drew a quick breath, clenching her hands. 'Have you told Max yet why you married me?'

'No,' he exclaimed grimly, 'and you'd better not either. She believes it was something which happened on impulse, because you bear a faint resemblance to how she once looked, long ago.'

'And she would never believe I was able to hold your interest?'

'I'm afraid not.' Again his glance travelled the length of her slender body, the pale, anxious lines of her face. 'Max has changed. She is quite a woman, even if she has no longer your extreme youthfulness.'

'She—she has more experience.'

'By far.' Putting down the brush, he put his hand

under Maxine's chin, turning her face up to his taunt-ingly. 'Rosebuds might be sweet, but one need never be so careful of the rose in full bloom.'

Maxine jerked her chin away, which didn't seem to please him. 'I don't want to listen to your stupid com-parisons, Kurt.'

'Be careful!' in his voice was a taut stirring of anger. 'Those who call me stupid, Maxine, have lived to regret it. Fortunately few have.' Drawing her closer, before she moved away from him, his hands went deviously under her robe to explore her smooth shoulders, the hard angle of his jaw daring her to protest. With a shudder she stood very still, feeling the bitterness go out of her, wanting only, in spite of what he thought, to melt against him, to feel his mouth on hers.

When he pushed her robe away with his hands, she quivered again. Through thoughts which were beginning to whirl she wondered why he liked looking at her when he hated her so much. She heard the callous satisfaction in his voice as he spoke to her. 'I'm not too stupid to know you aren't indifferent to me. If you persist in arousing my anger, you could be sorry. If I liked, I could soon fan your very responsive emotions into flames. I could have you begging to be in my arms, in my bed. On our wedding night....' Suddenly he stopped, drawing a deeply furious breath. With beads of perspiration on his forehead, his eyes came alive with a glinting anger.

'Tiens,' he cursed, whipping her thin gown back over her shoulders, thrusting her away from him, 'I must be going crazy! Since the first time I saw you....'

As his voice thickened, he paused abruptly, flicking his dark hair back with an unsteady hand.

'Kurt,' Maxine murmured his name, no more co-herently than he had finished his last sentence. Vaguely she knew that though he had come to her room, he had never intended touching her. And when he had spoken so savagely of their wedding night it had been no carefully rehearsed speech he had been delivering but something dragged from the depths of his soul. He had been startled, perhaps cynically, but whatever he had discovered of his feelings she could see it had only succeeded in making him angrier than ever.

Taking no notice of the desperate appeal in her eyes, he turned grimly from her, speaking half over his shoulder as he left the room. 'I am dining out tonight, so you don't have to dress unless you wish to. If you like I will tell Madame Lange to bring you a tray, then you can go early to bed.'

CHAPTER EIGHT

DURING the next few weeks Maxine saw little of her new husband. Occasionally, after dining with her, he would spend an hour talking to her, but more often, if he wasn't going out, he would disappear to his study where she dared not disturb him. To Madame Lange it must have seemed a very strange sort of marriage, but Maxine was grateful that she said nothing. Through the day Maxine helped the woman as much as she could but there was really little to do as there were too few people in the flat to cause untidiness.

Maxine passed the time in exploring the city and its shops. It was the largest city in Morocco, she had learnt, with the largest port and commercial centre. It was supposed to be white, but many of the buildings , she found, though Moorish in construction, were ochre or pink, or just a dusty concrete colour. It was, in fact, a modern city on an ancient settlement. Anfa, now a Casablanca suburb, appeared in the twelfth century, and the city itself had been occupied by the Portuguese and Moors as well as the Spanish and French. Over the centuries it had gathered importance because of being on an easy route to Marrakesh and gathering point for produce from the Sahara regions and the immediate vicinity, which was relatively rich and fertile. The port was large and busy and the world's largest phosphate exporting centre. Also there, she had discovered, were the factories of firms with many universally well known names.

Feeling driven to it, she tried discreetly to find out something of Kurt's business, but met with little success. The name d'Estier merely made people glance at her warily and seem unwilling to part with any information. There was the same respect she had encountered in the desert, but that, curiously enough, seemed to form a kind of blank wall which she couldn't penetrate. In the end she gave up and concentrated on things which disturbed her less, such as the shops.

Kurt insisted she was smartly dressed, although as yet he had introduced her to few of his friends. Many of the shops being fine and modern, Maxine knew she might have enjoyed buying new clothes, if her relationship with her husband had been happier. Eventually she had most of her new dresses made by a small dressmaker whom Madame Lange introduced her to. Maxine, uncertain at first, had her doubts dispelled when the dressmaker completed several beautifully styled gowns at a very low price. When she suggested she should be willing to pay more, Madame Lange shook her head.

'If you pay more she will expect it from everyone,' Madame cautioned sharply.

It seemed a strange philosophy to Maxine, but she didn't feel confident enough to argue. Privately she decided to have a word with Kurt about it, if she got the opportunity—and he would listen. Madame Lange, although a Moroccan, was half French and never believed in paying a penny more than she had to.

Maxine was wondering moodily when she would ever get an opportunity to wear her new dresses when Kurt surprised her. One morning, before she was up, he came into her bedroom.

'Don't disturb yourself,' he said, as she raised a startled, charmingly tousled head from her pillows to stare at him. 'We are going out this evening with Max and a friend. Have you done anything about your new wardrobe yet?'

'Yes.' Suddenly happier, she didn't remind him that it was he who had received and paid the bill. His indifference, since they had arrived in Casablanca, had amounted to what, in other circumstances, could only have been described as neglect. Was this invitation a sign that Kurt could be relenting towards her? It might not do to let him see what pleasure his invitation had given her, but she couldn't altogether subdue the sparkle of delight in her eyes as she continued looking at him.

'I'd like to go out,' she said shyly. Then, afraid she had betrayed too much, she asked, 'Who is this other friend? A man?'

'Naturally,' he replied dryly. 'Noel Franck, the man who came to me in the desert.'

'Who brought you the bad news....'

'The same.'

Max Martin must have taken up with him. What could be more natural when Noel held a position of some authority in Kurt's firm? Yet, if Kurt wasn't seeing Max when he went out most evenings, where did he go? Would she be foolish to think he had just been going about his business? Common sense refused to allow her to believe it but, for once, her heart won.

'I think you will like what I've bought, Kurt,' she smiled, sitting up straighter in the big bed, suddenly not caring that her nightgown revealed more than it managed to conceal. A decided wantonness swept through her, making her gentle grey eyes shine softly as she went on to tell him of the wonderful dressmaker she had found. Somehow this didn't seem the moment to confess the worries she had on this score. To have him with her for even a few harmonious moments was not to be threatened by something like that.

'Be ready by eight.' He had listened to her eager voice without impatience, even prompted her to talk longer by putting a question or two. As she paused at last he took his keen glance away from her with seeming reluctance. 'You'd better tell Madame Lange we won't be in for dinner.'

'Yes, Kurt.'

The wistful tone she used, as she sensed his imminent departure, brought the usual wariness back to his eyes. His mouth went hard and he spoke harshly. 'Next time I come into your room kindly cover yourself up. I don't accept the kind of invitation you're throwing out, not at this time of morning.'

He was a stranger again, Maxine's face went white rather than pink as she pulled her knees up to her chin, wrapping her arms around them protectively. Immediately he made her feel guilty. 'I'm sorry, Kurt.'

Into his eyes there sprang a glint of cruel satisfaction, but he merely shrugged as he turned away. 'You might check that my white jacket is back from the cleaners. Madame Lange is rather remiss about such things.'

For all he could hurt like the devil, it gave Maxine comfort to be able to do something for him. Time dragged as she was without the peace of mind which a stable marriage would have given. Often she felt suspended in a vacuum, floating in clouds of uneasy unreality, just waiting for the terrible moment when Kurt's final decision must plunge her to her death on the rocks of complete heartbreak down below.

To be able to go to his room, with his full permission, was like a ray of sunshine after weeks of rain, although she realised such a metaphor was idiotic in a country where the sun never seemed to stop shining. If anything she was rather surprised that Kurt should ask about one particular jacket, as he must have dozens. Madame Lange spoke of his tailor with considerable awe.

Venturing into his room was like entering the holy of holies. She had not been here before, had never dared to so much as peep in. Now she went cautiously with nervously held breath, wondering, with a shaken look on her face, what it would have felt like to have been able to sleep here beside him every night, as a true bride might have done.

In the middle of the bedroom, she stood quite still for a few moments, breathing in the faint, clean masculine tang which was so much a part of him, and which lingered tantalisingly even though he was gone. Her nerves tingling, she looked at the bed, very wide and long to accommodate his big masculine body. How many women had he entertained there? How many women had he held in his arms and loved, as he had loved his wife at the ksar?

Such a memory brought a choking sensation to Maxine's throat and she pushed it from her. Had he ever brought Max here, or some of the beautiful, exotic women she had caught glimpses of in the shops? She tried not to imagine his fine body, stretched out in the wide, shadowed bed, relaxed after a night of loving. Tried not to see him awakening in the early dawn to overwhelm the girl in his arms again with passion.

Her cheeks hot, Maxine practically dived into Kurt's wardrobe. This was what came from spending too much time alone, of dreaming too much of a man who didn't want her, who considered their marriage a mistake. The jacket was there, hanging with three others, and again she felt oddly bewildered. The wardrobe was full of elegant clothes, more than he could possibly use in several evenings. It didn't make sense that he had asked her to look out one particular jacket.

She was just about to give up and leave when her eyes fell on a small photograph standing on the dressing table. Something about it drawing her to it, she went over, picking it up. Taking it nearer to the window, she felt herself growing cold. It was Max Martin, and had obviously been taken recently. Maxine was in no doubt that this was what Kurt had intended her to see. His jacket had only been an excuse to make her aware he still intended marrying Max Martin as soon as he could. Across the bottom of the beautifully framed snapshot Max had written with a loving hand, 'In memory of the afternoon we spent yesterday.'

With a helpless gasp of agony, Maxine dropped the photograph and flinging herself on the bed began to weep.

By the time she was dressed she felt better. Her heart was still heavy, but a dull kind of resignation covered the worst of her pain. Kurt was perhaps being kind to leave her in no doubt as to his future intentions. The agony of knowing definitely that he and Max were spending time together would remain, but the shock of discovery could never come again.

Hearing Kurt come in, she didn't go to meet him but stayed in her room until she heard him go to his. After checking her face to ensure that there were no signs of the afternoon's copious tears, she went to wait for him in the lounge. It hadn't done to wonder wistfully if he might look in to ask how she was getting on, but at least he wasn't putting her out of his life completely. It was obvious now that he had asked her out to prevent immediate gossip about himself and Max, but nothing, Maxine felt, could be worse than having to stay in the flat almost every evening by herself.

She hadn't meant him to catch her watching the door, but it didn't seem to matter that he did. When he appeared the old saying, tall, dark and handsome, sprang to Maxine's mind, and she shivered with something very near excitement—an emotion, after all she had gone through, which she couldn't understand.

His eyes went over her very slender figure. 'You look charming, *madame*.'

His cynicism startled, but she was used to it. 'I've tried to do my best.' With determination she managed a grave smile.

'No doubt Noel will appreciate it,' he returned, very coolly.

Suddenly, with a returning feeling of hopelessness, tears sprang to her eyes. Ruthlessly he pounced on them. 'For heaven's sake learn to control yourself! If you're going to weep each time I speak sharply, you'll soon be doing nothing else. And talking of tears,' he added passively, gazing down at her strained face, 'I don't appreciate finding my bed in such a state. My pillow is soaked!'

Actually frightened, Maxine felt herself tremble. How could she have been such a fool? Madame Lange had been calling for her and she had had to rinse her face and leave the room in a hurry. She had forgotten to go back. 'I'm sorry,' she muttered miserably, the last shreds of composure dwindling before humiliation. 'I—I had a headache.'

'I didn't ask the cause,' he rejoined harshly. 'All I would ask is a little self-control. When two people are forced to live together it is necessary.'

God, didn't he have any compassion? Averting her head, she said dully, 'I'll see it doesn't happen again.'

He took her arm in steely fingers, but before he could say anything more, Madame Lange knocked to say that their guests were waiting.

They went straight down to join them. Kurt said it would save them the bother of coming up. Noel Franck was driving a long luxurious car, which must have cost many thousands, and Max was sitting beside him. Noel, whom Maxine had only seen once before but immedi-

ately recognised, didn't look altogether at ease beside his
attractive companion. He glanced at Kurt and his wife
with what looked suspiciously like relief. Maxine smiled
at him as Kurt put her in the back beside him.

They drove west, out of town, along the coastal boule-
vard, where huge breakers could be heard pounding
the jagged rocks of the Atlantic shore. Further on there
were many bathing establishments and opposite these
some of Casablanca's best nightclubs and restaurants. In
the city itself there was little social activity after midnight. The high old houses of the boulevards gave way to
the outskirts where they passed many new hotels. Noel
appeared to know the area like the back of his hand as he
drove swiftly and never hesitated.

Max leaned over the back of her seat, talking to Kurt,
who bent towards her attentively, all the time ignoring
his young wife who sat silently beside him.

They dined well, in a luxurious Moorish-styled nightclub, and afterwards danced. Maxine had eaten little.
Lately her healthy young appetite appeared to have
deserted her and she knew she was too thin. Even so,
the sight of so much food and wine seemed only to
take away her appetite, rather than increase it.

Noel, Maxine was discovering, was a very pleasant
man and he paid her a very flattering attention. She
wasn't sure how she could have got through the evening
without him. He wished to dance with her, after they
had eaten, and was so politely courteous about it that
she was grateful. It was as if he sensed some faint antagonism in Kurt and wanted to avert any repercussions
which might adversely affect Maxine.

'May I dance with your wife, Kurt?' he asked quietly.

'Certainly.' Kurt flicked a mocking glance at Maxine.
'Go ahead.'

Maxine flinched. Kurt must have known his voice was
totally indifferent. She wondered if he had made it deliberately so to hurt her. Lately he seemed to go out

of his way to do this, with the odd remark laden with
derisive undertones. He might well have announced
out loud that he had no interest in what his wife did.
During dinner he had scarcely spoken to her but directed
his conversation almost wholly on Max, who sat purring
like a contented cat. Maxine knew Noel was curious, but
he probably put Kurt's neglect down to a lovers' quarrel.
She in no way attempted to enlighten him as she danced
in his arms. Clearly Noel felt sorry for her, and this was
enough to make her squirm. It was a relief that, after
only knowing her for so short a time, he didn't feel
confident enough to offer sympathy.

But when he took her back to the table, after the
dance finished, and neither Kurt nor Max were anywhere
to be seen, Maxine's look of stark anguish moved him
to exclaim. 'Do not be so sad, *mademoiselle*—my apologies,' he hurried on, 'I mean *madame*. You look so young
I forget. Kurt will surely be here in a minute.'

Making a great attempt to pull herself together, Maxine murmured, 'Of course,' but was unable to get rid of
the anxious feeling of being deserted. Rather desperately
she smiled, 'You have known Kurt long, *monsieur*?'

'Call me Noel,' he begged, his eyes approving of her
courage. 'Yes, I have known him for many years. We are
much the same age and I work for him.'

She was surprised; she had thought him older. 'I'm
sorry I didn't get an opportunity to speak to you at
the oasis,' she faltered, uncertain as to whether she
should be mentioning the oasis at all. Noel's eyes were
kind, it might be too easy to talk to him.

'It was scarcely a time for making new acquaintances.'
His gentle smile removed any hint of reproach, and in
spite of his words, Maxine sensed he was now more
interested in herself than in the news he had brought
that day.

Because she couldn't stop thinking of Kurt, especially
when he didn't appear, she found herself asking questions

about him—questions which she realised must make Noel wonder why she hadn't asked Kurt himself, but which he was disposed to answer lightly.

'Kurt's parents were both French, but he was born here, as was his father. If he has little actual Moroccan blood in his veins, Morocco does possess all his loyalty.'

'He told me he is part Berber.'

'Yes, through an ancestor of long ago, but he never forgets. He does much for them. He does indeed devote much time to helping the poor of the country, no matter who they are.'

'All his spare time?'

Noel smiled, 'A little to his *amours, madame*, I will admit, although,' he hastened, 'it must be different now he is married. He is a man attractive to women, you understand.'

Maxine understood only too well. Didn't her own heartbeats refuse to dispute his virile attractiveness, though she tried hard to ignore it.

A waiter came up and passed Noel a note. As he read it his mouth tightened, in a way which reminded Maxine faintly of Kurt. 'What is it?' she asked anxiously.

'I——' he hesitated, with some embarrassment, 'Perhaps you'd better read it yourself, *ma chère*.'

'I'll take your word for it.' Suddenly Maxine couldn't bear to look at it. What was Kurt doing, writing her notes?

'Yes, well,' lowering his eyes to the paper again, Noel frowned, 'it appears that he and Miss Martin have gone elsewhere. He asks me to take you straight home.'

'Oh, no!' Maxine's face went white and she couldn't prevent her startled cry.

With a flick of his hand Noel waved the waiter away. 'Do not be too upset, Maxine,' his voice was gentle. 'All lovers quarrel, if only for the pleasure of making up. I can't say I approve of what Kurt has done, but he might have good reasons. Unfortunately he is unused to having to explain his actions, especially to a woman.'

'But I'm his wife. . . .'

'Yes,' Noel agreed, looking strangely helpless.

Then, before Maxine could stop herself, it came out. 'It was a mistake, our marriage. He doesn't love me.'

In bed, later that evening, she still felt she had been foolish in confessing the truth. She must have been wrong to let bitterness loosen her silly tongue. Yet her heart did feel comforted by the quiet sympathy she had received. She hadn't told Noel everything, but it had eased her mind to feel she wasn't quite so alone any more.

Noel might be loyal to Kurt, but Kurt's wife appealed to him in quite a different way. She was small, gentle and quite lovely. He wanted to protect her. Instead of taking her straight home, as Kurt had requested, he had insisted she had more coffee and that they dance again. No good would come, he had said, of lying in bed ceaselessly worrying.

Time had passed, and to Maxine's surprise it was two hours later before they had arrived back at the flat. Going into her room, she had fancied she heard a faint noise from Kurt's, but dismissed this wearily as imagination. It didn't do to let him haunt her so realistically.

Noel had been right, she thought as she undressed; to be tired and miserable was better than just being miserable. Getting into bed, she slept almost immediately, which must have been what he intended.

Unfortunately Noel's soothing therapy was soon dispelled by Kurt at breakfast. He rarely joined her at breakfast; she didn't think he had ever done so. Usually he was gone long before she got up. This morning, thinking he would be gone, and feeling tired, she trailed out in search of a cup of coffee wearing only a satin negligé. She was startled beyond everything to find him sitting in the kitchen pouring what looked like his second cup. He was dressed for the office but hadn't yet put on his jacket. He was immaculate, as usual, but looked tired. Angry unhappiness throbbing through her, Maxine wondered how he and Max had spent the night. He made no effort to disguise that he had had little sleep. Didn't he have any conscience whatsoever about a wife who—who loved him?

As she was about to beat a quick retreat, his cold voice jerked her back as he lifted his head and saw her. 'Don't go. I want to talk to you.'

'Why?' Maxine didn't turn around.

He rose, the noise of him pushing his chair back alarmingly loud, bringing her quickly around to face him. With two long, pantherish strides he reached her. He reminded her of how he had been in the desert, all dominating male, bent on having his own way. Quickly he took hold of her, pushing her down in the chair he had vacated, while he sat on the table, one hand resting on the scrubbed surface as he bent over her.

'You were late coming home last night,' he said.

There was a small, pulsing silence. Maxine trembled but forced herself to look at him. 'How did you know?'

'I heard you come in.'

Sheer astonishment kept her silent for a second. So she hadn't dreamt the small noise from his room. Yet why should she feel guilty? 'Well, what about it?' she stared up at him provokingly. 'I can't see how you can complain when it was you who was guilty of bad manners.'

'If we had been a normal husband and wife, yes. But we aren't.'

'But you said that everyone must be made to believe we were.'

His handsome face was implacable. 'I suppose Noel is responsible for this new aggression? I shouldn't have left you with him.'

'It's a bit late to think of that now, isn't it?' she retorted. She was rather pleased with her own coolness, but had to spoil it by adding, 'I think you've a nerve to say anything at all, when you went off with Max.'

'I was back over an hour before you were,' he replied curtly.

Startled, her eyes blinked before his. 'You were?'

'Max had a headache.'

Somehow Maxine couldn't believe it. Max had flirted with Kurt too blatantly to allow a mere headache to deprive her of her obvious objective. 'Oh, well,' she laughed with bitter flippancy, 'you can't win 'em all. Even I know that!'

'What's that supposed to mean?' he demanded impatiently.

'It doesn't matter.'

'Maxine, if there's one thing I dislike it's people who keep on telling me it doesn't matter, when I don't know what the hell they're on about!'

His sudden anger alarmed her, making her stiffen at his tone. She didn't think he would ever speak to Max like that. She sighed, not realising he heard. Kurt was a busy man, he had lots to do. Surely he hadn't waited this morning just to tell her she was stupid? He hadn't been with Max last night, they must have quarrelled, so why wasn't he hastening to her side with his apologies? Why was he lingering here, risking Max's disapproval when he hadn't tried to hide how much he wanted her?

A tremor of unhappiness shook Maxine as she considered what she was about to lose. The day stretching endlessly before her seemed more than she could face with only these thoughts for company. 'Kurt,' she pleaded impulsively, 'couldn't you find me something to do? I can type.'

He laughed, without amusement. 'You're my wife still.'

'Which means I can't work?'

'Definitely not, *chérie*.'

Never could she recall feeling so hopeless. Incensed, she cried, 'If you were a proper husband, Kurt, you would find me something to do.'

'If I were a proper husband,' he taunted, 'I would find other ways of keeping you occupied.'

'How?' she muttered mutinously, thinking he was talking of some of the good causes Noel had told her Kurt supported. It seemed too much to hope he would tell her about them, so she tried to hide her quickening interest.

Her mind fixed on some charitable occupation, she was unprepared to find him rising to his feet, drawing her up and swiftly to him.

'You ask the most foolish questions,' he mocked. 'This way,' he murmured, as he slid a searching hand under the thin satin of her negligé and his mouth found the softness of her lips.

'No!' Maxine wrenched herself away from him, terrified of the torment which ran through her. Kurt didn't want her, he only wanted to punish her, again and again.

She tried to get away, but felt him grasp her hair, a thick handful of it to pull her head back against his shoulder. He held her struggling body against him as he kissed her mouth again, cruel, deliberate kisses which had her reeling with anguish, yet aghast at her own response.

He was aware of this because he looked down at her with fiendish little lights in his eyes, reading the desire which shone in hers so clearly. Maxine's eyes were honest, she couldn't hide the way he could so easily make her feel. His long fingers moved across her cheek, then down the side of her neck while she watched him helplessly.

His mouth dropped to the corner of her quivering lips, sensitively coaxing. 'Maxine,' he muttered, huskily, 'you warm the blood in my veins to madness, you make me want what I can't have.'

Her head was spinning. Caution warned her that he was only amusing himself, that this was part of his revenge, but the clamouring of her own needs silenced the whispering voice of danger. Heavily her eyes closed, her head tilting back as their lips met on a tide of mutual passion. Turning fully to him, she put her arms around his neck. Tensely her fingers raked through his dark hair, urgently she clung to him, lost in mindless desire. Recklessly she gave him back kiss for kiss, feeling herself growing more dazed and submissive.

His hands were touching her hungrily, running restlessly over her, as though torn between a growing need of her and the hard common sense he could usually rely on. His muscles tensed as she pressed softly against him and his eyes smouldered darkly as his burning glance devoured her. 'Maxine,' he groaned despairingly, 'do you know what you're doing?'

Maxine could feel her pulse beating so fast she couldn't speak. She wanted to pull his head down again, to feel her mouth crushed again under his. She wanted to plead with him to do what he liked with her, yet his hoarse query slowly penetrated the hazy realms of her brain, convincing her she was acting immodestly. She pulled away from him, but his hand was still around her waist. She could feel the warmth of his strong fingers refusing to let her go.

They were still so close she could see each small line on his face, the sensuous curve of his disciplined mouth, the thick, dark lashes which half hid the blue eyes which looked down on her. She could not help closing her own eyes. She felt dizzy.

His breath shuddered, she could feel his heart pounding as his arms tightened and he began to pick her up. It was then that Madame Lange interrupted.

She stared at them curiously, as she came through the door, like a bright little bird but without embarrassment. Love was something Madame Lange understood. If she was bewildered, Maxine knew it was because she was unused to finding Kurt here at this time of morning. Nor would she be used to seeing him making love to his wife.

Maxine's cheeks were hot as Kurt put her down again and grew hotter still as Madame Lange asked tartly if neither of them had heard the telephone. 'Miss Martin wishes to speak to you, *monsieur*. Will I tell her you are engaged?'

'No. There is no need.'

He went to answer, pushing Maxine almost savagely aside before striding past Madame Lange, out of the kitchen.

Madame was not easily shocked. As she surveyed the disarrangement of Maxine's negligé, she said coyly, as she reached for the percolator, 'My late husband always said morning was the best time.'

Biting her lip, Maxine began retying her sash with hands which were not yet quite steady.

Grinding fresh coffee, Madame added, 'I don't know why Monsieur should give me such a killing look. He knows I come in at the same time each day, and it is my duty to answer the telephone, if everyone else is otherwise engaged.'

'We won't talk about it, if you don't mind,' Maxine was surprised to hear herself replying firmly. As Madame Lange sighed and then shrugged, she wished she could share a little of her resignation. How was it neither Kurt nor she had heard the telephone? She supposed it was simply that they had both been stupidly carried away. She could feel herself still quivering to the depth of her stomach, still feel the imprint of Kurt's strong body pressing there. Why did he torment her so? He must know how vulnerable she was, yet he persisted in arousing emotions he had no intention of satisfying.

What had he been going to do if Madame Lange hadn't come in when she had? Probably he would have taken her to her bedroom, thrown her on the bed and laughed

at her. The haste with which he had gone to answer
Max's summons confirmed this. He would never risk
spoiling his chances with Max.

Maxine eyed the kitchen door, which he had pulled
tightly shut after him, not sure what she would say to
him if he came back. He didn't. Madame Lange, singing
idly to herself, set about making coffee, then, as they
drank it, they heard Kurt leaving the flat. Madame Lange
glanced at Maxine's stricken face and began talking of
something else.

The rest of the day proved uneventful, apart from a
letter from Mrs Martin. Unable to stop thinking of
Kurt, Maxine was thankful for anything which might
divert her thoughts, even for a few minutes. She had
written to Mrs Martin soon after she had returned to
Casablanca. In her letter she had expressed her sympathy
about Colin and told Mrs Martin briefly of her marriage
to Kurt. It had been difficult to write at all, but she had
felt she must tell her something.

Mrs Martin hadn't replied until now and she was
extremely reticent. On practically the same line, she
said Colin's death had been a shock and she hoped
Maxine's marriage wouldn't prove disappointing.

Staring at the letter, Maxine shook her head unhappily. Kurt seemed to have left both of them without
anything to say. Mrs Martin did add that if Maxine ever
wanted her old job back she was welcome. Max, she
finished, was in Casablanca and settling well, but she
didn't know yet what she would do about the business.

Maxine didn't know what to make of the letter. While
in parts it was ambiguous there seemed something rather
pathetic about it. Colin's death must have completely
shattered Mrs Martin, whether she realised it or not, yet
Maxine knew she could never go back to her. It would
be much too painful, for one thing. Mrs Martin had used
her, perhaps not intending that Maxine, because of this,
should finish up married to a man who disliked her, but

Maxine could never trust her again. Besides, once away from Kurt, she wanted nothing which would continually remind her of him.

She didn't see Kurt again that day, nor did he get in touch to give her any idea of what he was doing. It was after midnight when she heard him come in, but although she had decided to pretend to be asleep, he never looked into her bedroom. The next morning she got up early, but he was gone and another day stretched drearily in front of her. If she didn't get something to do soon, she would go mad!

Convinced of this, she was more pleased than she might otherwise have been when Noel rang. He asked how she was, and if she would have lunch with him, almost in the same breath. Maxine hesitated, her first thought always being of Kurt. Then, realising he wouldn't care what she did so long as she was discreet, she agreed. Noel knew Kurt didn't love her, which made her feel she was going out with a friend.

Ordinarily she wouldn't have bothered much, but for her pride's sake she felt she must make a special effort. Kurt must have dined with Max last night and, after that, spent some hours with her. He couldn't object to his wife and his manager having an innocent meal together.

Noel took her to a very nice restaurant in the city. It was obviously one of the best and she was glad she had taken the time to make herself look attractive. She wore one of the smart little gowns her new dressmaker had finished for her. It was a soft, creamy white voile and she had narrow, four-inch heels which flattered her slender legs and arched her small feet elegantly. Her hair she had brushed until it shone, then pinned it in a thick coil at the back of her head. The heavy fairness of it made her neck look very long and slender and gave to her young face a delicate, more mature beauty.

Noel, as if he couldn't help himself, took her hand

and kissed it. He told her she looked charming. They had met in the foyer and, as he bent over her hand, Maxine found herself thinking how nice he was. She wondered why he wasn't married. Kurt had told her he was single.

Before they left he asked if she would dine with him later in the week and she was surprised to hear herself agreeing. She had had no intention of going out with him regularly. Maybe twice couldn't be termed that, but she sensed he was attracted and felt wary.

Just as they were ready to go, with Noel wishing ruefully, and audibly, that they had had the whole day, Maxine looked up to find Kurt and Max Martin standing beside them. Startled, she felt a guilty pink creep to her cheeks, but to her relief Kurt was smiling, if a little thinly.

'Can we join you?' he asked, although Max was clearly not keen.

'We're just leaving, I'm afraid,' Maxine stammered, conscious of his glinting eyes all over her.

'Oh, too bad,' Kurt replied indifferently, taking in his wife's enticing loveliness. 'Another time, perhaps, Noel?'

With a careless nod of his dark head, he took Max Martin's arm in an intimate clasp as they moved off, leaving Maxine staring after them in unhappy confusion.

CHAPTER NINE

TWICE more in the course of the next few weeks Maxine lunched with Noel Franck and had dinner with him frequently. For Noel's sake she tried to restrict the number of times she went out with him. He would have taken her somewhere every day, but she knew she could never return the feelings he was beginning to betray towards her. Yet she found it difficult to refuse his invitations altogether when Kurt saw more and more of Max Martin.

She was aware it must be public knowledge that their marriage was a failure, although people still accepted her as Kurt's wife. She had met many of his friends, several had asked them to dinner and been quite charming to her. Surprisingly Kurt had asked if she would mind if he returned this hospitality, and the party she had given had proved a great success. Mrs Martin had done some business entertaining and had trained Maxine well as to how to go about it. For once Maxine felt grateful, when she caught Kurt's look of appreciation as he realised she was quite capable of receiving his guests and keeping them amused.

Not having dared ask him not to invite Max Martin, Maxine had dreaded the moment when she would have to welcome her. To her astonishment Max hadn't turned up, but because of the relief she had felt, she hadn't asked Kurt why. She had pretended, instead, that Kurt hadn't invited her, even while she knew it must be something else which kept Max away.

Soon Maxine had more invitations than she could cope with, but it was a while before she realised they were mostly for during the day. Perhaps once a week she and Kurt would dine with some of his friends, but it was as if they knew he was usually otherwise engaged of an evening and had decided to be discreet.

None the less, it was gratifying to know she was making some small impact of her own in Kurt's circle, most of whom were of various nationalities as well as Moroccan. It gave her a faint glow of pleasure that she was becoming quite sought after, and if she would have exchanged everything and everyone for a desert tent and Kurt's love, she put on such a brave face that no one ever guessed.

No one perhaps but Noel. One night, after being out with him, she was unable to sleep. For the first time in weeks he had talked to her seriously, putting things which she liked to pretend didn't exist into words.

They had dined in a nightclub where the lights had been too low and intimate. Not for many of the other patrons, who were obviously lovers, but dangerous for those such as Noel and herself.

Maxine knew her uneasiness had been justified when Noel spoke. 'I've fallen in love with you, Maxine. I know it's no good. You love Kurt.'

'Yes,' she had agreed. There was no use denying it, but her face was despondent.

'Oh, *chérie* . . . !'

'Don't, Noel!' She had spoken quite sharply and hastily withdrawn from the hand he put out to lay over hers. 'I—I don't think it would really help to talk about it.'

'But this is what I want to do—help,' he had insisted, his kindly face shining with anxious adoration. 'Maxine, *chérie*, you're surely lovely enough to satisfy any man, yet he ignores you.'

'Noel!'

'But he does, Maxine. I don't know why.'

'Please, Noel,' she had pleaded, suddenly weary, yet thinking how right he was. Kurt did ignore her. It seemed a long time since he had come near her, and she had such a yearning for more than a few polite words.

'Never mind, *petite*,' Noel had sighed, his eyes compassionate. 'Perhaps you'll be able to tell me about it one day. One day you might be free.'

'Perhaps,' she had replied, dully, secretly wondering how soon that time would arrive.

'Doesn't he ever talk about it?' Noel went on, despite her protesting glance. '*Tiens*, I work for him. He has one of the best brains in the country and drives himself endlessly. For this I admire him. It is his treatment of you which arouses my contempt. He neither wants you nor will let you go. However did you come to get married?'

This she had promised Kurt not to confess, and even without such a promise it would have been too painful to put into words. Quickly, her face white, she had jumped to her feet, begging Noel to take her home, for once not listening to his plea that the night was still young.

It was still young. This must be why she was so restless and couldn't sleep. What Noel had said had stirred pain, but this she was well used to, so it couldn't be that. It made her uneasy to know without doubt that he loved her, but she knew it was something she had suspected for some time. Nor did the thought of having Noel to cling to, after Kurt divorced her, fill her exactly with dismay. He was good and kind and she could do worse, and he might not always work for Kurt.

No, it couldn't be Noel. With a sigh she got up and went to the kitchen, making a hot drink which she carried back to bed. The steam from it tickled her small nose as she set the mug carefully on her bedside table before looking for a book. With determination she tried to read.

The soft glow of the lamp played over her shoulders, shining on the pages, yet they constantly blurred as unhappiness swept over her in waves. Where was Kurt? What was he doing? Was he in Max Martin's bed, laying the foundations for a future in which she, Maxine, had no place?

She didn't hear Kurt come in. He must have, she thought with a frown, a way of entering the flat very quietly, as she couldn't remember the last time she had heard him come in. As it was only midnight she was surprised to hear him moving around in his room. He appeared to be doing a lot of it. There was the sound of doors closing, the creak of something she couldn't identify, water running as a tap turned.

She took a deep breath, wishing he would go to bed. How did he suppose anyone else was going to sleep when he made such a noise? She saw him removing his shirt, taking a shower, a towel wrapped around the waist of his powerful body. She took another deep breath which almost ended, this time, in a cry of defeated protest. His skin was supple and firm and he always looked like some pagan God. Dear heavens, why could she not simply forget him!

Her eyes closed, then opened wide as her door opened and he came in. She didn't reproach him, as she usually did, for not knocking—she didn't even think about it. Contrary to what she had thought, he looked as if he had already been in bed as his chin was dark with tomorrow's growth and his hair was ruffled from its usual thick smoothness. It looked as if he had been running moody fingers through it. Certainly he didn't look like a man who had been dining out with someone he loved.

Maxine didn't speak and, after her first startled glance, her eyes refused to go higher than his chin. To her surprise he came right up to her bed and removed the book from her hands. 'Maxine,' his lips twisted, as if he doubted his own common sense, 'I'd like to speak to you.'

'If you like.' She hadn't meant to shrug so carelessly, but who did he think he was, striding in here, demanding attention when she had scarcely seen him in days?

She saw, because her gaze was fixed on it, his jaw tighten. 'I won't have my wife speaking to me like that!'

'If I'd been your proper wife——' she began hotly, then paused warily. It was no use taking this line with Kurt. He was arrogant and had his own forms of reprisal. She might be wiser to hear him out quietly.

When she fell silent, he smiled tauntingly. 'So all I have to do to get your respect is to treat you as a proper wife? I remember you as a nervous virgin, *chérie*, but now perhaps you are that no longer? I know you respond to me, *mignonne*, it's no use trying to pretend you don't.'

Flushing scarlet, she clenched her hands until the nails bit into her palms. 'Please,' she begged in a low voice, 'what did you want to speak to me about?'

Kurt frowned, as though he had forgotten. 'Ah, yes. Very well. It is about Noel. You are seeing quite a lot of him, Maxine.'

'It's entirely harmless,' she cried, then felt her head drop guiltily.

'I wonder?' His eyes rested intently on her defensive figure. He might have been realising for the first time how very thin she was. 'Noel seems to wine and dine you enough, yet you do not look as if you eat the pricey meals he buys you.'

She let a heavy fall of hair continue to half hide her face. 'If I ate everything I'd get fat.'

'I doubt you'll ever be that, and I don't like you looking as though a wind might blow you away.' He sighed shortly. 'Maxine, I want you to promise not to see Noel for a while.'

'Are you concerned for me or him?' she asked dryly.

'He is a normal man, Maxine. At work he is brilliant, invaluable to me, but he is fast losing his powers of concentration. We have several important deals coming up and I need him.'

We—he must be referring to himself and Max Martin? A shaking agony prompted Maxine to cry recklessly, 'If you'd hurry and divorce me, perhaps I would marry him, then all would be well.'

Kurt straightened slowly, his eyes narrowed to glinting slits. 'Maxine,' he said harshly, 'stop making jokes.'

Jokes? Dear God, what did he expect? Hadn't he any idea what he was doing to her? The sickness he was making in her stomach, the need of him and his love which she longed for but he denied her. Wasn't he aware of how much she longed for him, while he stood over her, cheapening even the little there had been between them with a few thoughtless words? As a painful, primitive yearning took hold of her she almost moaned aloud. 'Should I think it a joke,' she choked, 'when you spend so much time with Miss Martin? If I feel like seeing Noel, I will!'

With a hint of savagery he retorted, 'You don't love him, Maxine. Why ruin another man's life?'

Kurt was angry. She felt afraid of him, yet had to ask, 'The other man being you, I suppose?'

'*Mon dieu!*' He ran impatient fingers through his hair. 'How you twist a man's words! I try to offer a little advice, for everyone's sake, and what do I get?'

Suddenly, without warning, she burst into tears, helpless tears which she tried to hide. Her nerves were ragged. She had an aching sense of loss and felt emotionally drained, but the last thing she'd wanted was to break down in front of Kurt. Never had she felt such inner turmoil. It was tearing her to little pieces, and she only wanted to be alone. 'Please,' she sobbed, burying her wet face in her hands, 'please go away!'

'Maxine!' The sight of her tears seemed to shake him. His jaw went tense. With a harsh exclamation he came down beside her, gathering her up in his arms. 'Don't,' he murmured thickly. 'Anything else I might stand, but not your tears. Surely Noel hasn't come to mean so much to you?'

'No....' About to confess that Kurt himself was the only one who mattered, she stopped short. It would only embarrass him to tell him this, yet she hadn't the strength of mind to push him away. His arms were comforting and comfort was one of the things she yearned for. Comfort and love, but if the latter wasn't available then the other would do.

She was very small in his arms. For a few minutes he held her, just letting her weep, not asking what she had been going to say. Forgetting about Noel, Maxine was only conscious of being with Kurt. Being in his arms fulfilled all her immediate ambitions, even though she knew all he felt for her was a fleeting compassion.

His shoulder was soaked, she could feel the hard muscle under her cheek growing damp and warmer. 'I'm sorry,' she gulped, making some attempt to regain control, while still reluctant to leave him. For long years Max Martin would have him, she couldn't begrudge his wife a few blissful moments.

'Maxine?' His chest heaved on a deep sigh. He shifted her weight a little, lifting her wet face so he could see it more clearly. 'Are you so miserable?'

Blindly she shook her head, like a child. 'Women cry at the least thing.'

His voice was soft. He went on regarding her closely. 'Somehow I think your problem is bigger than that. Perhaps it would help to talk about it. Is it because I took you into my bed, then neglected you?'

Only a man like Kurt could be so frank. In spite of her tears colour edged its way to her pale cheeks. Afraid he might suspect she loved him, she settled for half truths, which might prove more convincing than an outright lie. 'Maybe—in a way,' she mumbled, then added, with a helplessly innocent candour, 'It's something I don't really understand.'

Wryly he smiled, his fingers pushing back a cloud of gold hair from off her hot forehead. His movements were careful, meant to be consoling, his mouth even tender as he gently lowered it against her wide, smooth brow. 'You don't have the experience to understand, *ma chérie*, but I don't want Noel to be the one to enlighten you. He hasn't the finesse to love you as you should be loved, nor the depth to satisfy your passionate nature. I found you enchanting, Maxine, and you will be even more so.'

His words stabbed her, making her tremble. He had a nerve, reminding her of that, when he had scarcely

spared her a kind glance since. Noel might have his
faults, but he was no hypocrite. 'Noel is kind,' she said
tersely. 'You didn't want me, Kurt.'

He went quite still, then laughed softly, holding her
firmly as he felt her stiffen away from him. The struggling movements of her slight body might have excited
him. Or it might have been anger which brought the
dull flush to his face. 'I am very capable of wanting you.
A beautiful woman can drive a man mad, especially one
he is holding like this. You shouldn't underestimate your
own attractions, *mon chou*.'

Was this what she had been doing? His glance, suddenly burning, devoured her. The blood pounded through
her veins. She was terrified of her response, but she just
didn't know how to manage him, or, come to that, her
own feelings. She longed to stay in his arms, to beg him
not to leave her, but that would be too dangerous. If
she pulled them both deeper into the mire of their senses,
he would be the one to walk away unscathed. She
who would be left drowning in the sea of her wayward
emotions, in a worse state of unhappiness than before.

Yet it was already too late. While her mind pondered
and was afraid, her body reacted feverishly. Unconsciously her arms moved to his wide shoulders. She began
to cling, lifting a hand to touch his cheek, his hair. The
tips of her fingers slid downwards, lingering on the curve
of his mouth, ardent with longing.

She heard him say thickly, as he put up a hand to
switch off the light, 'Don't be frightened, *chérie*. I
won't go too fast this time. You will see I can be gentle.'
His mouth left her brow, reaching her ear, the sensitive
area below it, while she lay in his arms shaken and helpless. With a swiftly indrawn breath, which told of her
weakening resistance, Maxine's grip tightened at the
back of his neck, and she turned her lips to meet his.

He didn't move to reciprocate what she blindly pled
for immediately, but edged her gently back against the

pillows, all the time his gaze on her submissive face. She tried to look at him, but tears and sensuous emotions made her lethargic, and the smouldering flame in the depth of his eyes impossible to meet. As her heavy lids fell he searched beneath her long gold hair to push the narrow strap of her nightgown off her white shoulders, so that his mouth might explore the pale hollows of her satiny skin.

Dreamily, lulled by his gentle caresses, she relaxed as he stretched out beside her. He leaned forward, brushing aside the sheet that covered her, his hard, arrogant features softening as he stifled her sob of entreaty with his mouth.

As the moments lengthened a reckless feeling of pleasure swamped her. She closed her eyes as passion drove her nearer to him, losing all sense of time and consequence. Their mouths, parted and hungry, explored each other as her body leapt with erotic sensation.

She felt the fire and urgency of his kisses deepen and grow hot. His body crushed against her, forcing her down to the firmness of the mattress. Fiercely his hands gripped her, sliding to the slight swell of her hips as he felt her avid response. Each part of her lifted, curving to him. Her recollection of the first time he had made love to her might have created a barrier, but desire was too strong. Aware that her clinging arms and lips must be urging him to take what he wanted, she could feel no shame.

He talked softly in French, his voice low and persuasive, this and his passionate kisses removing the last of her resistance. His mouth moved over her until she felt almost desperate, her hands and fingers digging into his broad back, alive with wanting him.

'I can't let you go,' he said hoarsely. 'When I touch you, Maxine, I go up in flames. I want you, I must have you!'

Some of the tenderness was gone, his dark blue eyes

held a certain cruelty and his mouth was suddenly bruising. Her hands locked behind his head and again the nerves in her stomach jerked as he released inside her a primitive response. When he kissed her she was no longer in control of her emotions. The strong bones of him were an agony and delight, the hardness of his mouth a torment. As waves of passion swept over them she could no more struggle against him than she could a marauding sea.

'Kurt, darling....' She hadn't time to wonder if it could be her own voice begging weakly, before she was washed under, submerged, drowned in a vast ocean of mindless abandonment.

At ten-thirty next morning Noel rang, arousing Maxine from a heavy sleep. Before she was properly awake, her hand reached for the receiver. She heard him ask teasingly, 'Not still in bed?'

The jerk with which she sat up must have startled him. The line crackled as he asked abruptly, 'Darling, are you all right?'

'Yes.'

'Now you sound wooden.' He paused, as if forcing himself to speak lightly, 'What's going on this morning, *petite*? Kurt came in looking like murder. I've been keeping out of his way, I might tell you, but there are others who haven't been so lucky.'

'What did you want, Noel?'

'What ...? Oh, yes. I wondered if you would like to have lunch with me.'

Because it seemed the quickest way of getting rid of him, she agreed. He named a restaurant and she put down the receiver.

She sat staring at the white telephone for a full minute before dragging herself to the bathroom, under the shower. So Kurt was in a rage? What a fool she had been to hope that he might feel differently about her this morning. The water from the shower ran softly over her skin, where she could still feel the touch of his mouth. She couldn't remember falling asleep, or of Kurt leaving her bed, but when he had done so he must have been cursing the devil which had driven him there in the first place.

Having forgotten that Kurt had asked her not to see Noel again, she thought now it was the best thing to do. Kurt's mood, as described by Noel, seemed to prove how much he regretted spending the night with his wife. He would be relieved to know she wasn't sitting at home waiting to reproach him with it. Poor Kurt, she reflected bitterly, with a wisdom which had grown overnight, he wouldn't be the first man to be caught by circumstances which had somehow got out of control. It must be up to her to convince him that his wife had too much pride to even so much as mention what had happened.

While a small voice whispered that he had found a deep satisfaction in her arms, another voice told her firmly that this was merely wishful thinking. It was clearly certain he was filled with regret, otherwise wouldn't he have woken her, before he had left for the office, if only to reassure her? No, he had simply been affected, as any man might have been, by a few tears and a pair of clinging arms. For herself it had been quite different. She loved him, love had been behind the passionate response he had aroused in her, but Kurt would believe she had made a deliberate attempt to trap him.

Sighing, again on the verge of foolish tears, she stepped from the shower, reaching for a thick towel. Carefully she dried herself, then dressed, choosing something which was too elaborate for a simple lunch but which supplied her with a little Dutch courage. It took a lot of make-up to hide the dark shadows under her eyes, but she went easy with the lipstick on her sore mouth. As Madame Lange was having the morning off, there was no one to consult before she left. In the hall, however, she found a note from Kurt. He said he was sorry but he wouldn't be in to dinner as he had made previous arrangements to dine with a friend. This friend, Maxine knew, would be Max Martin.

It was almost one when she met Noel. They lunched together, but she didn't enjoy it. She might have done if she had been able to stop thinking of Kurt. Kurt beside her, kissing her, making love to her. Wearily she realised he was becoming an obsession.

Her dull depression failed to respond even to Noel's anxious cajoling, but it did make her forget the passing time. After they had eaten Noel took her for a drive along the shore to Anfa where they drank mint tea at another restaurant and watched the huge breakers rolling up the Atlantic shore. It was almost five when Noel dropped her at the flat. To her astonishment Kurt was at home.

All day Maxine, since reading his note, had felt miserable because she wouldn't be seeing him. Now she found herself wishing desperately that he had stayed away. She would have welcomed a chance to pull herself together, and this she hadn't had while she had been out with Noel.

Bracing herself, she lifted her chin to meet his disapproval, as he asked grimly if she had enjoyed her lunch. 'Where else did Noel take you?' he snapped, positively glaring at his wristwatch.

'Along the coast.' Her eyes dropped from his glinting ones to the fine gold watch strapped firmly over the dark hairs on his lean wrist, and her breath caught.

'I've been waiting some time.'

'What for?' she whispered. 'You left word you wouldn't be in. I thought you'd be dining with Miss Martin.'

'That's off,' he said roughly. 'We have somewhere to go, you and I.'

'Where, Kurt?' She could see he was in a peculiar mood, and felt suddenly frightened. He was pale, his eyes glittered, he seemed to have murder on his mind. She remembered this was the way he had looked on the morning after their marriage, when he had discovered she wasn't the girl he had thought he had married. Of course he would be annoyed because she had disobeyed him and gone out with Noel, but this surely couldn't have put him in such a rage. If things had been different she would have been here, in Kurt's arms, after last night, yet while she longed to be there she could see it was his intention to pretend that last night had never happened. 'Where are we going?' she asked again.

'We are going to the desert.'

'The desert?'

Her startled dismay must have shown, for he stared at her grimly. 'You have been there before, *madame*.'

'Oh, Kurt!' Suddenly, impulsively she ran to him, laying an entreating hand on his arm. It seemed incredible, after the hours he had spent in her room, through the night, that they should be speaking to each other like strangers. But as soon as she touched him she drew back, aware that some things weren't so easily put right. 'I'm sorry,' she whispered, her face white, then red with mortification.

He considered her embarrassment coldly. 'I shouldn't say anything you might regret, and I refer to actions as well as words. My friends in the desert have heard of my marriage and naturally wish to meet my bride.'

Shaken and bemused, she couldn't drag her eyes from him, wondering what kind of a man was this, whom she had married. It might help if she could see him belonging in one definite niche. In the desert, where she had first known him, the role of a Berber tribesman had sat easily and convincingly on his broad shoulders. Here in Casablanca he seemed even more convincingly a hard, international, cosmopolitan business man, bent on wringing the best deals from life, especially when it came to marriage. He confused and dismayed her, yet she only loved him more and wanted the best for him. Her heart concentrating on this, she began, 'If you take me to meet them, will you ever be able to divorce me?'

'Not easily,' he snarled, the anger she dreaded glittering afresh. 'You saw to that with your tears and entreaties last night, did you not? It is an old trick, one I stupidly fell for, but if you are so determined on a loveless marriage then you must be prepared to assume the full duties of a wife.'

Stunned, Maxine faltered, her grey eyes darkening with anguish, 'Duties, Kurt?'

His full, straight mouth, which could be so sensual, hardened. 'Social duties, *madame*. One day we might escape the mess we find ourselves in. Until then we must —how is it, you say, make the best of it.'

'I see.' Her eyes fell. She couldn't look at him, his face was a cold, savage mask. When the doorbell rang she felt almost grateful.

With a muttered curse he went to answer it, Madame Lange not being in. It added to Maxine's despair when she saw Max Martin stepping inside.

Miss Martin halted, glancing quickly from one to the other, her face nearly as unfriendly as Kurt's as she stared at Maxine. It wasn't at all unfriendly as she turned again to Kurt. Ignoring his wife, she went up to him. Sliding both arms around his waist, she gazed up at him appealingly, looking straight into his eyes. 'I wanted to speak to you, Kurt. After what you told me at lunch, I thought you wouldn't mind if I came here.'

'Of course not, *chérie*.' Putting a gentle finger under her chin, he tilted her deep red mouth, kissing it lightly, '*Cela m'est égal, ma chère.*'

'Kurt!' Maxine whispered.

Hearing her low protest, he raised his head, but instead of responding to the hurt in her voice, he told her harshly to be quiet. '*Tais-toi!*'

Taking Miss Martin's arm, he smiled at her, then said to Maxine, 'You must excuse us.'

Maxine watched dully as they went to the lounge and closed the door. She noticed the door didn't close completely, but felt too paralysed with misery to do anything about it. She could hear Kurt talking quietly, but Miss Martin's voice was suddenly raised. Quite clearly Maxine heard her say. 'When will you tell her, Kurt?'

'I'm not sure, but I have definitely made up my mind that we are finished. During the next few days I will think of the best way. I don't want to hurt her any more than is necessary.'

Her heart thudding heavily with anguish, Maxine fled to her room. Nothing made sense any more, but it was clear that Kurt was making final arrangements to get rid of his marriage. Yet why was he arranging this crazy trip to the desert? He spoke of not wishing to hurt her in the same breath as he did of getting rid of her. Hadn't he any idea of how she felt? If he was trying to make the final break as gently as possible it showed he wasn't entirely without consideration, but no matter how he did it, he could never soften such a blow.

After Miss Martin left, a few minutes later, he came to find her. She didn't ask what Max had wanted to speak to him about and he made no comment. His temper didn't seem improved, but she hadn't expected it to be, not after overhearing the conversation in the lounge.

'Pack a few things,' he frowned as he caught her standing listlessly in front of the dressing unit. 'There should have been someone here to do it for you—a servant.'

'I can manage,' she laughed lightly, in order to hide how she was distraught. 'I've often wondered, though, why you don't have hordes of servants here, like you have at the ksar.'

'It's different here. In a bachelor flat they aren't really necessary.'

'Perhaps not,' she agreed carefully, averting her face. 'How long will we be gone, Kurt?'

'A few days. A week maybe.'

'We'll be coming back here?'

'Yes.' He shot her a quick glance. 'Why do you ask?'

Again the necessity to take a deep, steadying breath. 'If you still think it's a good idea to take me to see your —your friends, then I must know what to take. The— the first time, remember, I arrived with far too little.'

'Must you remind me of that?'

'No.' She almost apologised but stopped herself in time. She hadn't meant to remind him of anything. It had just slipped out. 'Will I want any dresses,' she persisted, 'or just a pair of slacks?'

'Slacks, yes.' Impatiently, when she made no effort to move, he opened the door of the wardrobe and began sorting through it. He threw out several long dresses followed by two short ones. 'You will have to take something formal,' he said, 'as we'll be spending the night in Marrakesh. It is now too late to go any further.'

A car took them to the airport. Nouasseur Airport lay some nineteen miles from the city. From here they flew to Marrakesh where another car waited to transfer them to their hotel. They might have been any normal couple, Maxine thought cynically, as Kurt had rarely spoken to her since they set out. He had been silent on the plane, busy all the time with what appeared to be business papers, but she didn't look closely. As she was still unused to air travel she found plenty of interest in what was going on around her. The only thing she found impossible to ignore was Kurt's nearness. Once or twice she even heard him sigh, and once when she moved her arm touched his, making her breath catch at the spark of fire which flashed through her.

She thought it likely that Kurt would simply go to

the first hotel he thought of and hope they had some rooms to spare. When the car pulled up before a smart, luxurious-looking building, she was surprised. At the reception desk they were obviously expected, so he must have made reservations. Yet when?

'I was sure you would like it,' he smiled faintly at her astonished expression. 'This is the best hotel in Marrakesh, some say in the whole of North Africa.'

Maxine did like it, or it might have been more truthful to say she would have liked it better if she had felt happier. Having puzzled all the way here as to Kurt's exact intentions, she had reached the bewildering conclusion that he might merely be playing with both Max Martin and herself. It didn't make sense that any man would consider a trip into the desert as a necessary preliminary to getting rid of his wife, or that a man with serious intentions towards another girl should seek to fob her off with such a story. He must think both her and Max Martin fools! Because of this Maxine felt her temper rising. She must find some way of making sure Kurt paid dearly for his ruthlessness. A little revenge might mitigate some of the pain he had caused. It was as she wondered how she could bring this about that she found herself floundering hopelessly.

They were given a complete suite of rooms with only one door leading on to the corridor. Maxine had never stayed in anything like it; the luxury was almost overpowering. Again her surprised expression appeared to amuse her husband.

He made no comment, however, but indicated towards one of the bedrooms. 'You'd better have that one. I know how a woman can dither if she's given a choice, and I'm too hungry to wait much longer for my dinner.'

'Yes, Kurt.'

'The shower will be over there. You won't have time to take a bath.'

'I suppose you know how a woman can dither in that, too?'

He glanced at her suspiciously, but she met his blue eyes innocently, smiling coolly. 'If you don't mind,' she murmured, 'I think I'll do with a quick wash and shower later. I feel hungry, myself.'

'Just as you like,' removing his narrowed eyes, he turned away. 'Ten minutes, then.'

Her bedroom was like some boudoir out of the Arabian Nights. It was luxuriously furnished and comfortable in the extreme, but Maxine allowed herself little more than a quick glance around before beginning to dress. Off came her blue cotton pants and silky top, her brief cream satin cami-knickers. Quickly she washed, wishing she hadn't decided against a shower. Ten minutes later, exactly, she was ready.

CHAPTER TEN

THE dress she wore was brown and gold with a slight glitter to the filmy material. The little dressmaker in Casa had insisted it was the latest thing. So, too, she had said, was the low neckline, but Maxine gazed at it doubtfully. It seemed too low, and she felt she would have been much happier with something higher. She could only hope that Kurt would be so used to seeing women in sophisticated clothes he wouldn't notice. Her hair she caught in a thick coil on top of her small, graceful head, with only a few loose, shining strands escaping. As at lunch she used quite a lot of make-up, hoping this and her dress would draw Kurt's attention from her pallor.

'You look lovely, *ma chère*.' Kurt, extremely good to look at himself, took her arm as they went down to the restaurant. He surprised her by adding teasingly, 'We make a handsome couple, don't you think?'

Maxine knew she wasn't tall enough to compare well with Kurt's height and breadth, but she couldn't suppress a small thrill of pleasure. In spite of the animosity between them, there was also a kind of tense awareness which left her hungering for, and appreciating even a few kind words.

The service in the restaurant was quiet and good, the food excellent. They ate well. Maxine was coming to love Moroccan cooking. The herbs and spices which were used made an incredible difference to the plainest of dishes. They had some French dishes, too, of which there was a great variety. She finished with fruit while Kurt had cheese. During the meal, as though to make up for his neglect on the plane, Kurt talked a lot about Marrakesh, his eyes only occasionally leaving Maxine's absorbed face to linger on the depth of her cleavage.

The hotel had a nightclub, and when Kurt mentioned it she asked if they could go for a while. The wine she had drunk with the meal, and Kurt's kinder attention had taken the edge off her unhappiness and apprehension. The immediate past and future receded, leaving a more pleasurable glow. As the evening progressed she found to her surprise she was enjoying herself. Yet when Kurt suggested it was time to retire, she found all her tension returning.

Nevertheless, not able to think of a plausible excuse to linger longer, she didn't demur.

Upstairs, Kurt was close behind her as they entered their suite. As he closed the door he asked abruptly, 'Are you going straight to bed, Maxine?'

'I think I will,' she managed a careless little shrug while avoiding his intent eyes. 'It seems to have been quite a day.'

He smiled tightly, and seeing his better humour fading, she wished she hadn't reminded him. 'I hope,' he said, 'you made no further plans to meet Noel?'

Deliberately she laughed, recalling her resolve to stand up to him. 'At least he doesn't come chasing all over the flat!'

'You mean Max, of course?'

'Yes.'

His eyes glinting with anger, he turned on her, 'Maxine...!'

'Please, Kurt,' she interrupted hastily, 'don't. Don't let's spoil what I think has been a pleasant evening. I'll say goodnight.'

In her bedroom she lay half panting against the door, wondering at the ease of her escape. The force of his personality when he was displeased always made her feel battered, but she had no wish to provoke him into anything.

Breathing a sigh of relief that he made no attempt to follow, she undressed and took a shower, putting a cap over her hair to prevent it getting wet at this late hour. Wrapped in her dressing gown, she went back to her room, smelling sweetly, her hair, free of the shower cap, a loose cloud over her shoulders.

Her heart jerked as she found Kurt lounging on the bed, resting sardonically on a pile of pillows he had pushed against the deep, quilted headboard. Her fingers clenching nervously, she paused in the doorway. 'Did you want something, Kurt?'

'Only you,' he smiled tauntingly. 'This bed is as big as mine, so I will be just as comfortable here.'

Now her heart raced. 'You must be joking!' she cried.

His dark brows rose as his eyes flickered over her. 'Ah, yes, I understand. No, *mon chou*, I am not pretending for the fun of it—to alarm you. You are my wife.'

Maxine stared at him, her colour mounting. Hadn't she heard him telling Miss Martin he wanted rid of her, but

didn't want her hurt? He was choosing a funny way of
going about it! Last night—yes. That had been something which had just happened. It hadn't been intentional; Kurt had confessed as much himself. But to come
here, to her room, was deliberate. 'I don't understand
you,' she breathed.

His mouth twisted indifferently. 'I'm not interested
in whether you understand me or not. I only want you
to....' Surprisingly he broke off, but he couldn't, she
felt sure, have been going to speak of love. 'Never
mind,' he shrugged, as with a lithe movement he was on
his feet, by her side, picking her up. Holding her tightly
in his strong arms, he looked down on her startled face.
'Am I always to be pleading with you, girl? Don't you
ever wish to come to me of your own accord?'

Before she could find words to protest, he had lowered her to the bed and begun removing her robe. 'Stop
it, Kurt!' she found her voice at last as she tried to
push him away. 'Don't you know what you're doing?'

'Most certainly, *chérie*.' There was a warm, sensual
intensity in his eyes which sent the blood flowing wildly
through her veins. 'I wouldn't be much of a man if I
didn't.'

'Well, let me go, you beast!' His face swam before
her, and she knew if she didn't get rid of him quickly
her own desire might leap to meet his. Already her body
was responding urgently.

'*Non, ma belle*,' his white teeth glinted as he held her
fast, 'don't goad me. I will have you, whether you like
it or not. Haven't you been tempting me all evening?'

'You'll only make me hate you more.'

For a moment he went rigid, then with a small harsh
sound he caught her closer, seeking her mouth with his.
His dressing gown was open, their bodies touched and
ecstasy consumed Maxine as his hands roved over her.
For a dizzy moment, with his mouth forcefully demanding, she lay quite still, dazed by the great waves of excite-

ment which washed over her. Then she was clinging helplessly, exchanging kiss for kiss, until passion and desire drove out everything but their urgent mounting need of each other.

Next morning Maxine stirred with the dawn to find Kurt sleeping peacefully beside her. Wonderingly she gazed at him. This was the first time she had seen him like this, and she thought he looked younger. Greatly daring, she raised herself on one elbow. Only a sheet covered the bottom half of his body. It did little to disguise the powerful lines of it. She had to visibly restrain herself from caressing the dark, silky hairs which covered his bare chest, as she had done an hour or so ago. She had an urge, which she knew to be shameful, as he hadn't long been asleep, to put her arms around him and waken him with soft little kisses. But, through the night, although he had drawn a mindless response from her, he hadn't been particularly kind, and she thought twice about arousing him so soon.

Turning over quickly, she slid quietly from the bed. Covering herself with her robe, she went out on to the balcony. The hotel was near the wide walls of the city and the sky was slowly lightening. Down in the garden, and beyond the walls, in the palm groves, birds were beginning to sing, the first few notes a prelude to a great orchestra. Somewhere in the city the *muezzin* called the faithful to prayer, and was endlessly echoed by neighbours. Then the sun began to rise over the Atlas mountains, tipping the snow-covered peaks with crimson and gold, and the individual sounds began slowly to merge with the more general ones of the awakening streets.

Something immediately behind her made her turn quickly, but she was too late. It was Kurt. Kurt with her best cotton nightdress tied sarong-like around his waist, wearing nothing else but a wry smile. She tried not to look at the muscles which rippled in his powerful legs as he came towards her.

'You and the dawn beat me to it, child.'

'I must have remembered how I liked getting up early in the desert,' she rejoined shyly, some of the pink of the rising sun reflecting in her cheeks. Nervously she swallowed, unable to meet his eyes.

'So you are sampling now the delights of Marrakesh,' he sounded amused. 'I must show you more, later.'

'If you have time,' she agreed, not daring to betray her eagerness in case he was merely being polite. 'What time is it?' she asked, trying to disguise a weakness inside her which was responding urgently to his superb vitality.

'It is too early,' he grumbled, his eyes leaving the mountains to return to her body, reminding her tantalisingly of the madness they had shared in the night. 'Much too early, *ma belle*. Come back to bed.'

She wasn't sure if she had been going to object, but whatever it was it died in her throat as his arms closed possessively round her. His lips were suddenly fierce on hers, then with a smothered groan he lifted her, carrying her with him back to the wide, waiting bed.

At breakfast, which was brought to their suite hours later, Maxine was pale. This didn't appear to please her husband, who sat down to join her when the waiter had gone. 'You are not supposed to look pale and interesting until you are *enceinte*, Maxine.'

Prowling around, still undressed, he had the look of a sensuous tiger. She remembered his mouth against her throat, the hard strength of his male body. Taking in what he had just said, she felt herself flushing scarlet. He could be cruelly callous when he chose. 'You don't need to worry about that,' she returned bitterly.

'*Eh bien*, who is worrying?' he retorted impatiently. 'I merely wonder why, when you weren't exactly an icicle in my arms last night, you should be looking so distraught. Did I fail to please you, *chérie*?'

How easy it would be to hate him, if she hadn't loved him so much. How could he taunt her by asking that when he was so well aware of her passionate response. Lowering her fair head, she pretended to concentrate on her croissant, spreading it with butter then delicious cherry jam. The freshly baked roll was still warm and crusty and she shouldn't have been able to wait to get her teeth into it. Instead she stared at it helplessly, forgetting she was expected to eat it. How could she tell Kurt she couldn't ever forget what he had said about being married to a nobody?

Unhappily she whispered, 'I'm sorry, Kurt.'

Lifting her head to look at him, she was startled to see an expression of tenderness crossing his face. She couldn't recall seeing it before. It softened his harsh features, making him seem almost approachable again.

He halted his restless prowling. Getting rid of his coffee cup, he came down by her side. Putting a gentle arm around her slender shoulders, he drew her carefully back against him. 'It's I who should be sorry, *ma mie*. You are pale because you are not used to having a man in your bed. Perhaps,' his eyes glinted wickedly, 'we should stay in this morning. It's almost noon now, anyway.'

As his arms tightened, she pulled herself frantically away from him. 'Please, Kurt,' she gasped furiously, 'I think this has gone far enough. You can either show me Marrakesh or take me to the desert. I just want to finish what we came to do, then go home. And this time I mean England. One thing is certain, I won't be going in any more bedrooms with you, not ever!'

Too late she regretted her impulsive speech, yet as he put her roughly from him she could see no possibility of changing her mind. If all Kurt wanted was a little fun, he shouldn't continue having it at her expense.

'Get dressed, then,' he said grimly, his jaw taut with anger. 'I will show you the city, if you think you can still enjoy it, and tomorrow we will visit the oasis. But keep this in mind,' he added savagely, 'if I feel like coming to your room, I will. You are my wife, *ma belle*, and, as I have already told you, I don't intend you should forget it.'

When Maxine had passed through Marrakesh, when she had first come to Morocco, she had wished she had been able to have a proper look around. She soon realised she might easily have got lost exploring on her own, and that Kurt made a wonderful guide. A guide with a far from smiling face, perhaps, but one who certainly knew his way around. They visited mosques and markets, palaces and tombs. They pursued endless alleyways with endless twists and turns, saw ruins and gardens and the city's encircling walls, a continuance of that which could be seen from the hotel bedroom.

In a French restaurant on one of the wide boulevards they ate a quick lunch—quick, Maxine supposed, because neither of them was disposed to linger. Kurt talked politely but was again a stranger, and her heart felt so heavy she knew she would never be happy again.

After lunch she asked if they could revisit one of the souks—the markets, where, with so much going on, it would be impossible to dwell on her own misery. The Djemaael-Fna seemed like a wonderful fairground, with dancers and snake-charmers, illusionists and story-tellers, but she also liked the market stalls. Here there were heaps of dates, sacks of grain, many things sewn up in skins, bottles of stuff which Kurt told her was rancid fat for cooking, pieces of meat covered with flies. Women sat on mats covered with gaudy articles, beads, trinkets, woven baskets and clothes. Leather goods abounded, many of them beautifully stitched and fringed. There was everything, jackets and handbags, the flat, moccasin-like shoes and slippers. On another stall she was fascinated by the large dishes of spices, the bunches of grapes and herbs, the dried figs strung in long ropes, the net sacks of various nuts.

'*Marbaba*,' one of the stallholders, a dark, stout woman, smiled and nodded at Maxine as she stopped to admire an attractive string of the most colourful beads.

Kurt told her this meant welcome. After a little light haggling he bought the necklace for her. He even draped it, with an ironical twist to his mouth, around her slim neck.

'Thank you,' she said shyly. Rather uncomfortably she glanced up at him through thick, curling lashes. 'It's been a wonderful day, Kurt.'

'I'm glad you've enjoyed it,' he rejoined coolly, placing a hand on her arm to guide her back to the wider streets. Here he hailed a car to take them to the hotel.

Despondently she stared out of the window while her smooth white fingers played nervously with the gift he had given her. The inflection in his voice had clearly indicated that he hadn't shared her enjoyment, and she wondered how much more she could endure.

Later that evening, after they had dined, he was called to the telephone. When he returned he said that a business colleague had a problem, and that he had agreed to see him on the following afternoon. This meant they would have to stay in Marrakesh another day, but, as he would have the morning free, he would take her to see something of the surrounding countryside.

That night, in spite of his threats, he didn't come to her room. Lying awake in the huge bed, Maxine found she missed him desperately.

This insidious feeling of being bereft persisted even after she got up, and as she dressed. She hadn't risked going out on the balcony to see the dawn, but she had seen Kurt's tall silhouette through the tinted glass of her window. She had been confused at the restraint it had taken to prevent herself from going out and joining him.

Kurt hired a car which was brought around to the

hotel but which he chose to drive himself. He had decided to show her the Ourika valley, which always reminded him of Switzerland, where occasionally he went to ski. The road was fairly new and fast, but he adjusted his speed so she could take everything in. The High Atlas villages Maxine found particularly interesting, especially those on the road to the Tizi n' Test pass.

They had lunch in a very good hotel at Ouirgane, in a beautiful green mountain setting, after which Kurt said they must return to Marrakesh, or he would be late for his appointment.

Looking at him, Maxine bit her lip. This morning he had been smiling and polite, but she hadn't seemed able to get near him. Perhaps it was better this way, as the empty hours through the night had proved how vulnerable she was, but she couldn't forget how much she loved him. Yet what sense was there in loving a man who only wanted to get rid of you? Wasn't he only using her to satisfy his immediate needs, and maybe some sadistic streak in his nature? As soon as he had satisfied the tribal customs of the people whom he apparently looked on as blood brothers, he would set about getting rid of the wife he was so arrogantly going to present to them. In such a way as would not hurt her! Bitterly Maxine regarded her tall, dark husband as he paid the bill for their meal and accepted what she thought was markedly deferential treatment from the staff. How, she wondered, did he intend doing this?

Kurt drove the car he had hired as expertly as he seemed to do everything else. Maxine, sitting quietly beside him, did nothing to break his concentration. She would liked to have asked questions about the different districts they were passing, but she guessed he was thinking of the man he was to meet. It was when they had almost reached the city that she did something she had never imagined she could ever do.

Staring blindly out at the approaching walls, her mind centred wholly on Kurt and his confusing way of going about things, she saw a man beating an old donkey. The poor animal was thin to the point of emaciation and the man had a large stick.

'Oh, Kurt!' Suddenly, without warning, she grabbed his arm and, because in that same second he had taken his other hand momentarily off the steering wheel, the big car shot straight off the road.

Afterwards it always made Maxine shudder to think she could have done anything so foolish. As the car left the hard surface, the scream of tyres combined with Kurt's warning shout came savagely to her ears. Things seemed to whirl past, in a nightmarish kaleidoscope of donkeys and sticks and big men. Of city walls, Kurt's incredulous face and stony sand. Then people shouting. Nothing was clear until the moment when she realised she was kneeling beside an unconscious Kurt crying, 'Darling, oh, darling!' over and over again.

It appeared she had been thrown clear while Kurt was trapped in the overturned car and had to be dragged free by a passing motorist. Strangely enough this man happened to be a famous London surgeon, who actually knew Kurt. He earned Maxine's eternal gratitude by declaring he didn't think Kurt was at all badly hurt. He hadn't been unconscious when the surgeon had first reached him and had been able to help fairly freely with his own rescue. A blow on the head might account for his subsequent concussion.

'Is he your husband?' The man, who had introduced himself as Alan Davers-Clarke, frowned as he stared at Maxine's distressed young face. His eyes went to the heavy gold band on her finger. As she nodded, he said, 'I had no idea he'd married.'

Kurt was taken to hospital but, after tests and X-rays, was allowed out the next afternoon. Maxine passed a terrible twenty-four hours. When the police had arrived on the scene, she had confessed that it had all been her fault. Not being familiar with foreign police she had thought they might either shoot her on the spot or haul her off to prison. She had been humbly surprised when they had assured her that as no one else was involved there would be no proceedings. They had been nice, extremely pleasant. They had treated her like royalty and begged her not to worry.

This only made her feel worse as she felt she should have been punished for what she had done. Instead, everyone was so kind. At the hospital, where they had firmly removed her from Kurt's side so they might examine him, she had tried to pull herself together and ring the hotel. She had taken what she had thought was the sensible precaution of booking their suite for another week. The staff here had told her that even if Kurt was sent out he would need several days of rest and quiet.

The manager of the hotel had come and spoken to her himself, assuring her, as the police had, not to worry. For Monsieur d'Estier he and his staff would do anything. Monsieur was an important man. Dazed, Maxine began feeling rather like a V.I.P.

Although badly shaken herself, she had stayed at the hospital all day. For a long time she had refused to leave Kurt, crying quietly over him as he lay so still and white, unable to stop. She had held his hand and whispered his name while tears had poured down her pale cheeks. Then they had given her a bed and made her rest, and the doctor had examined her, too. He had hummed and hawed, with little frowns and quick intelligent glances at her tear-stained young face, asking several questions which she had scarcely been aware of answering. When she had asked what was wrong with her, he had merely smiled slightly and replied that he didn't think it was anything to worry about.

She had been so worn out with despair that she had fallen asleep and when later she had woken, a nurse had given her a warm drink and told her that, if she liked, she could stay for the night. Maxine had asked to see Kurt again, but they had said he was sleeping soundly and would rather he wasn't disturbed. He was much better, however, and would almost certainly be leaving in the morning.

On hearing this, Maxine decided to go back to the hotel. It was only after nine, and if Kurt hadn't suffered any serious injury, there was no reason why she should stay—apart from her own silly personal ones which didn't matter. After what she had done Kurt would only be embarrassed by her presence, and it might do him harm to lose his temper at this stage of his recovery. It would be better to wait for him at the hotel where, by the time he reached it, he would be strong enough to give free expression to his rage.

To her surprise a nurse came with her and stayed all night, only leaving next morning when Maxine insisted she was all right. Apart from a slight uneasiness when she first got up she did feel better, and the nurse must have many more patients who were really ill to see to. After a light breakfast she put on a soft white dress and a pair of matching sandals. Then, after ringing the hospital about Kurt, she sat down to await his arrival.

All morning she waited anxiously, but it wasn't until well into the afternoon that he appeared. Hearing voices in the corridor outside, she knew instinctively it was he, but he entered the suite alone and closed the door.

Maxine raised her head slowly, her eyes wide with apprehension. He still wore a bandage around his brow. It reminded her of the haik he had worn in the desert. She stood looking at him, feeling sick with fright. He had a temper, she knew, she also realised she deserved everything he was about to say.

'I'm sorry I was so stupid, Kurt,' she got out at last, as the silence threatened to stifle her. If he didn't say something soon, she thought she would scream. The tension inside her had been building up all morning. He could have no idea how she had suffered over him. How she had just wanted to die, too, when she had thought she had killed him. She was still suffering from the shock of it all, like a festering sore which refused to heal. If he didn't speak to her it would prove irrevocably the strength of his hate. 'I—I don't suppose you'll ever forgive me,' she muttered miserably.

He completely dumbfounded her by looking almost relieved and sitting down, rather promptly. 'I'll most certainly forgive you,' he said lightly, 'if you'll find me a drink. I still feel as if I'd been hit with a bargepole, *chérie*.'

Rushing to do as he asked, she felt a crazy kind of joy that he didn't want to kill her. 'I thought you'd feel like murdering me,' she gulped.

'Yes, well,' his smile was faintly sardonic, 'I think I can just recall feeling quite murderous when you grabbed my arm, but who am I to complain when I'm really none the worse?'

'Oh, Kurt...!'

His glance falling from her anguished face, he took his drink from her soberly. 'I think I might have preferred to have been left a helpless invalid, *ma belle*, which might have kept you chained to my side for the rest of your life.'

Pain flickered in her eyes. 'You know you could never have tolerated that. Oh, Kurt,' unable to help herself, she knelt beside him on the settee, very young-looking in her simple, button-through dress, her fair hair now a tumbled, silky mass about her shoulders, 'I've been so worried! How do you really feel?'

'Well enough, apart from this crack on my head,' his eyes darkened. 'And you, *chérie*?'

'Me? Oh, I'm fine,' Colour touched her cheeks with a sudden glow, for his voice was kind. 'My tummy's been a bit upset, but I expect that was because I've been so worried about you. I'll be all right now.'

'I hope so.' His eyes went grimly over her. '*Mon dieu*, the risks you take!'

'It was that poor donkey, Kurt!' She hadn't dared mention it to anyone, not since she had explained to the police. 'A man was beating it cruelly.'

'It's quite a common occurrence, I'm afraid.'

Indignantly she moved back an inch. 'Well, it should be stopped!'

'Oh, Maxine!'

She wouldn't have believed she would be glaring at him so scornfully, within seconds of his leaving hospital. 'You'll be telling me next that the poor creature never felt a thing!'

'No,' he replied soberly, 'I wouldn't do that, but I think if you'd been able to see the whole thing you would have found that the donkey wasn't beaten over-much. It certainly doesn't appear to make much difference to their affection for their masters. In the U.K., Maxine, I've known people do worse things to their children and dogs. In a lot of people I believe there is some degree of cruelty, and I doubt if it could be got rid of completely. Not that it's excusable, of course.'

'I—I suppose you're right,' she agreed ruefully. Looking at him, she felt the familiar urge to touch him. For fear he should guess, she hurried on, 'The man who rescued you from the car said he knew you.'

'Yes, we're old friends, actually. He came to see me this morning. He and his wife are staying in Marrakesh for a few days and he wants us to dine with them one evening.'

'He seemed nice. I'd like that.'

'Would you, Maxine?'

Feeling the sting of tears, she nodded. They were like two strangers. She found it difficult to bear.

When he said softly, 'Maxine, I want to talk to you,' she could still only nod. Then noticing his paleness, she cried out in alarm, forgetting her tear-bright eyes, 'Oh, Kurt, do you think you should? I mean, you've only just come out of hospital, and if it's something which can wait. . . .'

'I'm afraid it won't—darling.' With an enigmatical smile at her suddenly flushed face, he reached over, taking her hand in his.

As suddenly she recoiled from him, with a swift sense of alarm. A fright which she realised was fully justified, as he went on remorselessly.

'Before the darkness of hell descended on me yesterday, *mignonne*, I seem to remember someone calling me darling, again and again.'

Closing her eyes quickly, Maxine prayed for composure. 'I—I was frightened, of course.'

'You don't deny it, then?'

Numbly she shook her head.

'I know many English girls use the word indiscriminately, Maxine, but I hadn't heard it from you before.'

She felt a miserable wave of jealousy. 'Just from—other girls?'

'A few,' he answered, with a wicked gleam at the mutiny in a pair of beautiful grey eyes. 'From them it meant little, and they knew what they were about. But I don't believe you would utter it unless you loved a man, *chérie?*'

Helplessly, knowing the time for denial had passed, she stared down at the wonderful oriental carpet which covered the floor. 'Perhaps not.'

She heard his deep sigh, even as his tug on the hand he held brought her tumbling against him, and the eyes which bore down into her distressed ones glittered with triumph.

'Perhaps not!' he echoed thickly. 'Is that the best you can do? *Tiens, ma mie*, do you not know how I've been almost out of my mind worrying about you? How, this morning, I refused to remain in hospital? The need to have you in my arms was too great to be ignored any longer. When I realised we might both have gone to our deaths with nothing resolved between us.... Oh, God, *mon amour*, it was to realise there are more fools on earth than could possibly be imagined!'

'You—you can't mean you love me?' Open-mouthed with astonishment, she raised her head to stare at him, only to find her breath removed in a merciless grip and her lips crushed under his until she felt the room fading. She heard him repeating hoarsely how much he loved her, felt his lips exploring her burning face, his hands undoing the buttons on her bodice. His damp mouth was on her bared flesh, arousing her swiftly as he held her savagely, as if intent on satisfying the passionate needs of his demanding body. He didn't have to speak of the intense hunger that drove him. She felt it, too, and reciprocated it, as everything inside her melted in a mindless dream.

Yet suddenly it wasn't enough. 'No, Kurt, wait!' Using what little strength she had left, she escaped from his arms and stumbled to her feet. She was weak and distraught, but things had to be right between them. He had said that he loved her, but was his love strong enough to override his initial contempt of her as a penniless orphan, his desire for a divorce? 'You were right,' she gasped, 'we must talk.'

He straightened, glancing at her quizzically, and she quivered, wishing she had some of his iron control. 'You haven't told me all I have to know....'

His eyebrows rose sardonically. 'I thought I was expressing myself rather well.'

She drew a quick breath at this. 'You've told me you love me, but since we were married all you've wanted was a divorce!'

'Not any more, *chérie*.' He rose, and before she could retreat he was beside her, his hand under her chin, his eyes, very sober now, fixed on her white face. 'I haven't wanted a divorce for some time, not since I came to my senses and learnt how much I loved you.'

'But you've told me so often,' she breathed, 'how much you hated me.'

'Not you,' he replied curtly. 'In fact I doubt if I ever really hated anyone. The blow to my pride, perhaps, when my fiancée went away with another man. The even worse one when I discovered I had married the wrong girl, but you aroused different emotions.'

He turned across the room, then came back to her, where she could still see his face. 'When a bachelor approaches his middle thirties, Maxine, he sometimes comes to the conclusion that he might do worse than get married and provide himself with a son and heir. The girl I chose was French, a wealthy widow of the aristocracy, without any children of her own. She seemed ideal. We had known each other many years. Then she met Colin Martin. I can see now that because I had no strong affection for her that I neglected her. I put business first and she had too much time alone. So—Colin and she fell in love and eloped. Thus the first blow to my regrettable pride. When you arrived, believing you were Colin's sister I decided it was fitting that you should suffer a little too. Hence our journey into the desert.'

'Didn't you ever suspect I wasn't the Maxine Martin whom you thought I was?'

He smiled, half in self-derision. 'I certainly know the difference now. But you do see, *ma belle*, it had been ten years, and you didn't exactly deny you were her to begin with. When I first met her, with her hair tinted, she did resemble you closely, but she never had your innocence. I soon began to find differences which confused me, but at the ksar, when you first arrived, I was too full of arrogance and pride to see clearly.'

Maxine felt she had to ask it. 'Didn't you fall in love with Miss Martin? She always implied that you did.'

He shook his head. 'No, I was young and impressionable, but she had a certain hardness which put me off. Then I found her with other men, once in circumstances I do not care to recall.'

Maxine said slowly, 'Yet you did marry her, or you thought you did. When Noel brought the news of the plane crash to the oasis, you still believed I was Miss Martin, although I tried to explain again.'

Pulling her close, Kurt threaded his hand through her hair, drawing her head against his shoulder. 'I know. I was too busy trying to convince myself that by marrying you I would not only achieve the perfect revenge, but also get all my mother-in-law's riches. My people in the desert are often poor, Maxine. This money would have helped them in many ways, but it was no excuse for making you suffer as I did.'

Somehow this didn't seem important any more, yet Maxine couldn't help asking curiously, 'If I had been Colin's sister, Kurt, do you think our marriage would have worked?'

'I was going to see that it did. Already I was amazed to find myself attracted to you, in a way I never remembered being before. I found myself unable to stay away from you.'

'Then you found out the truth. . . .'

'Yes,' his voice went harsh. 'You have no idea the rage I felt then. For the second time in a matter of days it seemed I had been made a fool of. And oh, *mon dieu*, what a fool! Yet pride was only the half of it. I hadn't been any too gentle, *petite*, but I thought I'd found heaven in your arms, on our wedding night. Pride alone forced me to deny this, to declare nothing would prevent me from getting rid of you. It was a thousand times worse when later I realised I was in love with you. The other night, when I made love to you again, I knew it was useless to go on fighting. My fate was sealed, my love. I went out early next morning, determined to have everything put right before telling you all this, but there were complications.'

Frowning a little, because she didn't understand, Maxine said, 'You left a note saying you—you were dining out?'

'It was foolish of me, but I expected I would be working. I should have been, but suddenly I couldn't stay away from you any longer. I decided to leave and take you to the desert. There I hoped you would discover you loved me.'

'Kurt,' Maxine swallowed quickly, 'did you ever tell Miss Martin you were going to get rid of me?'

'No, *chérie.* I said such things to you but never to her. There were times, too, when I was crazily jealous of Noel and said things just to hurt you.'

'But,' Maxine rushed on, knowing that if she waited she might never again find the courage to mention it, 'I overheard you talking to her in the lounge—the door wasn't properly closed. You said you'd made up your mind we were finished, but you didn't want to hurt me more than was necessary.'

For a moment he stared down at her, his face pale under his tan. 'Oh, Maxine,' he groaned, 'darling, I could have spared you that! I was talking about Mrs Martin, Colin's mother. I'm leaving the company I've been running for her. I have too many other commitments anyway. The government are taking over, and I have already put the necessary machinery into action. Mrs Martin won't lose out. I do realise, in spite of what I've said, that she must have suffered, and I mean to make things as easy as possible for her. Max is going home permanently, which should help.'

'I'm so glad.' Maxine felt tears touch her eyes again, but whether it was because of Kurt's compassion, or Mrs Martin, she wasn't sure. Perhaps both. 'Mrs Martin did ask me not to protest too much if you were to mistake me for her daughter, but I doubt if she ever imagined the situation would change as it did. She was always kind to me—a poor orphan,' she finished, with a teasing though slightly anxious smile.

He groaned again, against her warm neck. 'So I'm never to be allowed to forget calling you that, am I? Though, *mon dieu*, how I could have said it, loving you as much as I do, I just don't know?'

'And doing as much for orphans as you do,' she rebuked softly, her eyes full of tender derision. 'Noel has told me quite a lot about the time and money you give to them.'

'Don't mention that man to me!' he growled. 'I can still see the way he looks at you.' As if to punish her, he bent her back over his arm, kissing her until every nerve in her body throbbed with painful longing. Minutes later, ruthlessly surveying her glowing cheeks, he asked huskily, 'Maxine, do you love me enough to be able to forgive me and live here with me? You'd have to be prepared to share my life in the desert as well as the cities. I want you to bear my children, to be with me wherever I might have to travel. But most of all I want you to love me.'

'Oh, but I do, Kurt, I do!' Trying to steady her racing heart, she spoke fervently. Then she started, as he put a sudden hand to his head. 'Kurt,' she cried anxiously, 'you should be in bed!'

Smiling mockingly, he swung her up into his arms. 'I was merely preventing the bandage from slipping over my eyes, *mon chou*, but you could be right about bed. Feeling as I do about you, I can't think of a better place.'

Hiding her hot face against his broad shoulder, Maxine wasn't prepared to argue. It still seemed incredible that Kurt cared for her, wanted her, but amazingly he did.

'I love you, darling,' she whispered, as he made good his threat by carrying her straight into the bedroom.

He smiled gently and closed the door.

The Mills & Boon Rose is the Rose of Romance

Every month there are ten new titles to choose from — ten new
stories about people falling in love, people you want to read
about, people in exciting, far-away places. Choose Mills & Boon.
It's your way of relaxing:

September's titles are:

WHERE THE WOLF LEADS *by Jane Arbor*
Everybody seemed to behave like sheep where Dracon
Leloupblanc was concerned. And why, thought Tara Dryden
indignantly, should she add herself to their number?

THE DARK OASIS *by Margaret Pargeter*
When Mrs Martin's son ran off with Kurt d'Estier's fiancée, she
persuaded her secretary Maxine to go off to Morocco to try to
pacify Kurt.

BAREFOOT BRIDE *by Dorothy Cork*
To save face when she found her fiancé strangely unwelcoming,
Amy pretended that she was going to marry the cynical Mike
Saunders instead — then Mike stunned her by taking her up on
it . . .

A TOUCH OF THE DEVIL *by Anne Weale*
There was mutual attraction between Joe Crawford and Bianca
— but marriage, Joe made it clear, was not in his mind.

THE SILVER THAW *by Betty Neels*
A holiday in Norway was supposed to give Amelia and her fiancé
Tom a chance to get their affairs settled once and for all. But
somehow she found herself seeing far more of Gideon van der
Tolck.

DANGEROUS TIDE *by Elizabeth Graham*
Her ex-husband was the last person Toni had expected to meet
on board a cruise ship to Mexico. But he, it appeared, had
expected to meet her . . .

MARRIAGE IN HASTE *by Sue Peters*
Trapped in a Far Eastern country on the brink of civil war,
Netta could only manage to escape if she married the mysterious
Joss de Courcy . . .

THE TENDER LEAVES *by Essie Summers*
Searching for her father in New Zealand, Maria could have done
without the help of the disapproving Struan Mandeville. But
could she *really* do without Struan?

LOVE AND NO MARRIAGE *by Roberta Leigh*
Career woman Samantha swiftly fell in love with Bart Jackson,
who had no time for career girls and thought she was a quiet
little homebody . . .

THE ICE MAIDEN *by Sally Wentworth*
Just for an experiment, Gemma and her friends had computerised
the highly eligible Paul Verignac, and Gemma was proceeding to
turn herself into 'his kind of woman' . . .

If you have difficulty in obtaining any of these books from your
local paperback retailer, write to:

Mills & Boon Reader Service
P.O. Box 236, Thornton Road, Croydon, Surrey, CR9 3RU.

Mills & Boon Classics

The very best of Mills & Boon
romances, brought back for those of you
who missed reading them when they
were first published.

In
September
we bring back the following four
great romantic titles.

NO FRIEND OF MINE
by Lilian Peake

Lester Kings was her brother's friend, not hers, Elise told herself
firmly. She had never liked him when she was a child, and now
he had come back into their lives the old antagonism was there
still, as strong as ever. Yet somehow she just couldn't stop
thinking about him . . .

SHADE OF THE PALMS
by Roberta Leigh

To Stephen Brandon, Julia was no more than Miss Watson, his
unflappable, highly efficient secretary. A dowdy woman wearing
unfashionable clothes, sensible shoes and spectacles, he would
have thought if he'd considered the matter at all. But he was to
discover that appearances can be deceptive and that there was a
totally unexpected side to Julia . . .

THE BRIDE OF ROMANO
by Rebecca Stratton

It was the charming Paolo Veronese who had got Storm the job
of governess to the little Gino in southern Italy, but it was
Gino's stern guardian, Alexei Romano, who caused her all the
heart-searching. She knew that in getting involved with Alexei
she would be utterly outclassed, but all the same . . .

THE ARROGANCE OF LOVE
by Anne Mather

Dominic Halstad was the most attractive man Susan had ever
met, and made her rather difficult fiancé David seem dull by
comparison. But even if her first loyalty were not to David, what
right had she to think about Dominic — a married man?

Doctor Nurse Romances

and September's
stories of romantic relationships behind the scenes
of modern medical life are:

FIRST YEAR LOVE
by Clare Lavenham

When Kate started her nursing career at Northleigh
Hospital, she was thrilled to recognise the consultant
surgeon as a long-time friend of her brother's. Might her
childish hero-worship now blossom into something more
mature? Or was she looking in the wrong direction
altogether?

SURGEON IN CHARGE
(Winter of Change)
by Betty Neels

Mary Jane was over twenty-one, and a competent staff
nurse, so when she inherited a fortune she was furious
to find that she also had a guardian — the high-handed
Fabian van der Blocq. But what could she do about it
— or him?

Masquerade
Historical Romances

Intrigue
excitement
romance

CROMWELL'S CAPTAIN
by Anne Madden

Why should Cathie Gifford, who came of a staunchly
Royalist family, feel compelled to tend the wounded
Roundhead captain? And why should a man like
Piers Denham, who had betrayed his own kind by
fighting for Parliament, be able to shake her loyalty
to the King?

HOUSE OF SATAN
by Gina Veronese

Count Anton von Arnheim's Viennese mansion was
notorious, even in the pleasure-loving society of 1785.
And into it came Eloise, the Count's innocent and
beautiful ward. How long could she go on living
happily in the House of Satan?

Look out for these titles in your local paperback shop from
12th September 1980